BACKWATER COVE

A KURT HUNTER MYSTERY

STEVEN BECKER

THE WHITE MARLIN PRESS

**Get my starter library First Bite for Free!
when you sign up for my newsletter**

http://eepurl.com/-obDj

First Bite contains the first book in each of Steven Becker's series:

- **Wood's Reef**
- **Pirate**
- **Bonefish Blues**

By joining you will receive one or two emails a month about what I'm doing and special offers.

Your contact information and privacy are important to me. I will not spam or share your email with anyone.

Wood's Reef

"A riveting tale of intrigue and terrorism, Key West characters in their *full glory! Fast paced and continually changing direction Mr Becker has me hooked on his skillful and adventurous tales from the Conch Republic!"*

Pirate
"A gripping tale of pirate adventure off the coast of 19th Century Florida!"

Bonefish Blues*"I just couldn't put this book down. A great plot filled with action. Steven Becker brings each character to life, allowing the reader to become immersed in the plot."*

Get them now (http://eepurl.com/-obDj)

Copyright © 2018 by Steven Becker
All rights reserved.
No part of this book may be reproduced in any form or by any electronic or mechanical means, including information storage and retrieval systems, without written permission from the author, except for the use of brief quotations in a book review.

Join my mailing list
and get a free copy of Wood's Ledge
http://mactravisbooks.com

For those that like to follow along or are interested in the location of some of the key scenes in the book please go to:

https://stevenbeckerauthor.com/locations-in-my-books/
Here you can find interactive Google Maps

The Kurt Hunter Series

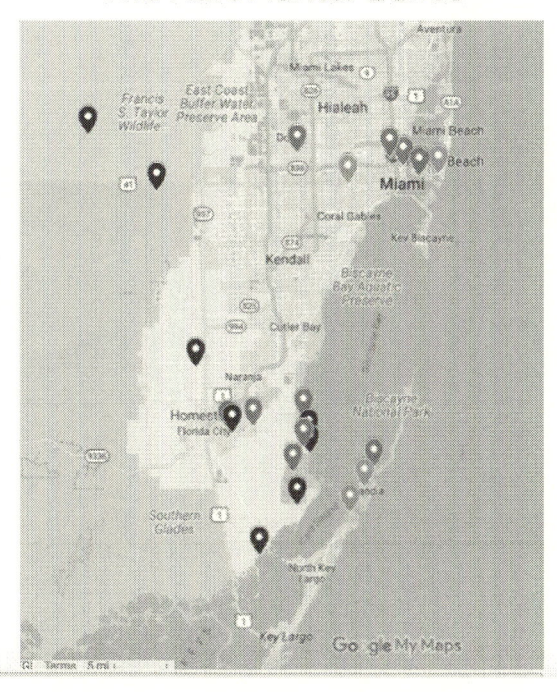

1

I sat on my back porch, watching what was being billed as the last cold front of the season pass through. There were sure to be more, but the natives claimed that February in South Florida was it for winter. Rain beat down on the metal roof covering the raised, screened-in patio while lightning flashed to the south. It illuminated my backyard enough to see the freshly cut grass. Although I lived on an island, my park service-issue house was inland and had no water views. That was fine with me. As a special agent for the Biscayne Park, I spent my days on the water. Sipping my beer, I watched the palm trees bend, fighting the north wind. The supple trees are hurricane resistant, with the trades generally out of the southeast, and the north wind rubbed against their grain.

It rubbed against my grain, too, which was surprising since I had spent most of my thirty-eight years in Northern California near the Plumas National Forest. At five thousand feet of elevation and a latitude that matched New York, we got a real winter there. Here in South Florida, fifty degrees had the locals in down coats and boots. I wasn't quite that bad yet, but anything colder than seventy-degree water felt unnatural. The sounds of the storm were interrupted by

Zero, my neighbors' dog, who sat at my feet snoring loudly. The way he sidled up to me, I thought he felt the same way.

My blood hadn't thinned to the point that I ran for the down, but I did have on a hoodie and decided to make the switch from beer to bourbon. I had just gotten off the phone with Justine, who got a good laugh out of my complaints about the weather.

Adams Key, the island refuge that Ray's family and I shared with the small day-use area kept me isolated, something that came naturally to me. It was harder to see Justine, but that was the only thing I missed besides my daughter. Thinking of Allie made me sad and I realized it had been over a year since I had spoken to her. I hoped to resolve that soon. For me, this job was kind of like the witness protection program of the park service. It was lonely when I had nothing but my routine patrols and Justine was at work, but we were well along to a commitment I never thought I would make again.

My life had been turned upside down a little over a year ago, when on a patrol in the Plumas Forest, which usually involved fly fishing the streams, I had found a hidden inlet to an irrigation system. Following it had led me to the largest pot grow ever found on public land. Things got ugly for my family when the cartel came after me. They did what they usually do and resorted to violence when I refused to change my testimony. The attack came in the form of a firebomb. Our house had been destroyed and the next day, I found myself in front of a judge at an emergency custody hearing. It didn't take a rocket scientist to figure out the outcome of that; I hadn't even bothered retaining a lawyer.

Allie was taken away by her mother. I had suspected they were now living near Orlando with Jane's sister. After nearly a year and with quite a bit of prodding from Justine, I had finally done something about it. A month ago, I contacted an attorney and finally made it onto his schedule for an appointment tomorrow. I was apprehensive about it and my expectations were low. I'd really felt like I was a danger to them after the explosion, but now things had settled down and if I could see her for a few weekends and holidays, I'd call it a win.

Just as I returned from the kitchen with my two fingers of bourbon, I realized the rain had stopped. Zero raised his head and cocked it toward the screen door. I downed half the drink and went to let him out. It wasn't a long way up for the pit bull mix, who always reminded me of Petey from the Little Rascals, but he made it to his feet and wandered to the door, waddled down the porch stairs, and sniffed the air before setting a tentative paw on the wet grass. I set my glass down, slid my cold feet into my flip flops and followed him onto the large lawn that separated the two houses on the island.

While he took care of business, I turned to Ray and Becky's house and saw what could have been the last weak flash of lightning before the storm tried to break the invisible tropical barrier to the Florida Keys, just to the south of the park.

Geologically, Biscayne National Park was the true beginning of the chain of islands stretching to Key West and beyond, but Key Largo, just to the south was the official start of paradise. It might have been the proximity of the park to Miami, just ten miles to the north, or the menace of the two chimneys of the Turkey Point nuclear power plant to the southwest that excluded us from the Keys, but we were what we were.

Zero barked and I turned to look over at Becky and Ray's house, hoping he hadn't woken Jamie, their three-year-old son. The house stayed dark and I assumed there would be no complaints if Zero stayed at my house for the night. After years of listening to him bark, they said that they were immune to it. I couldn't imagine that.

I heard him rooting around back in the mangroves to the north of the clearing where the two houses sat and called for him, hoping he hadn't gone too far into the brush. The island was small, only a few acres and mostly left to nature. The day-use area and the two homes were located on the well-manicured southern tip of the island. The large open area was unique to these islands; a left over from the old Cocolobo Cay Club. The Key was accessible only by water, and via a long concrete dock set into Caesar Creek. The well-traveled pass from Bayfront Park near Homestead took hundreds of boats a day past my front door. Zero barked at most of them, but now he was heading into the swampy interior.

I called for him, and heard him again, preoccupied by something. He started barking and after a quick glance at the dark house next door, I guessed it was up to me to figure out what he was up to.

Using my phone as a flashlight, I started down what would have been a game path, if there were any game out here. That wasn't exactly true. There were all kind of creatures living on these islands, including crocodiles. Bred out of the cooling canals at the power plant across the bay, the American Crocodile frequented these waters, but most somehow knew the boundaries of the Crocodile Lake National Wildlife Refuge located about twenty miles to the south in Card Sound where they were protected.

Once in a while, one found its way here, but not for long enough to create the well-worn path. My Alabama-bred neighbor would take care of that. I flashed the light toward the ground every few steps to avoid any bombs the creator of the path might have left and continued after him.

The track grew softer as I walked and I could see Zero's paw prints clearly now. They glistened in the moonlight and, with little water in them, I knew he had just passed. The ground turned to a quicksand-like muck as I continued, and every few steps I had to pause to pull my flip flop out of the mud. The rainy season had not really started yet, and the storm, although violent, had been like most of the cold fronts that made it this far south—short and hard. The ground I was walking through was a saltwater swamp, and I knew my feet and ankles would be laced with bites from the micro critters that lived here.

Trying to ignore my misery, I called after Zero. There was no response. He was intent on something and ignored me. Continuing after him, I soon found myself at the edge of the island looking across a short channel at Elliot Key. The three-mile-long island, along with Adams Key and several others on the other side of Caesar Creek, are loosely known as Islandia. Created by a group of ambitious developers in the 1930s, they had never gotten much further than dredging a few deep-water canals that led to nowhere and building a small club here. Originally, Adams Key had been named Cocolobo Key and Islandia had a nice ring to it, but like most of the get-rich-quick schemes so common in South Florida, it had failed as well. Whatever was still standing in 1992 had been destroyed and washed out to sea when the eye of Hurricane Andrew, packing 150-mph winds, passed directly over where I stood.

Cursing the dog and the swamp, I continued, now following only the sounds of his movements through the bush since his paw prints were no longer visible in the ankle-deep muck. I heard him stop and start snorting. My hand went to my belt, searching for my gun. It wasn't there and, again, I cursed myself. There was nothing good in a swamp at night.

I heard a strange noise, almost like a whisper that I tried to separate from the rustle of the palm trees. Whatever it was, it was faint and I stopped, trying to eliminate any unrelated sounds. The wind was still blowing, making it hard to discern if it were really a human. The only way to find out was to move forward.

The voice became more clearly defined as I approached. It was definitely human and as I moved closer, I could tell it was a woman. If Zero hadn't been there, I would have figured her for crazy, but I soon recognized her nonsensical words as the baby talk people use with dogs. There wasn't enough light to make any kind of evaluation of her. If she was armed, the last thing I needed was to barge in and get shot. If she wasn't, I didn't want to scare her. I announced my presence by calling for Zero.

Purposefully, I rustled the branches of the mangroves as I approached to let her know which direction I was coming from. I reached the last bush and saw her bent over the dog, talking to him in her singsong voice. It took a few minutes for her to notice me, and when she looked up, I saw her tear-streaked face.

"Name's Kurt Hunter." I stood five feet from her with my hands in my pockets, not wanting to appear threatening. "I'm a ranger out here." I preferred ranger to Special Agent, my actual title, in many circumstances.

She slowly rose. "My name's Misty," she said.

Her voice broke when she tried to talk.

"Misty, do you need some help? Are you alone? Are you hurt?" I asked, trying to keep the questions to a minimum, but I had a lot of them.

"I'm kind of okay, and yes, I'm here alone."

She was clearly not okay by the look of her. Wearing a torn sundress that looked expensive even to my uneducated eye, she was wet, covered in mud, and trembling. "I live out here. Why don't you come back to my place and we can get you cleaned up and see if we can find your people?" Only a brave person would be out here alone in a storm at night. She didn't look that brave and she was dressed for a party, not an expedition.

She nodded and took a step toward me. I wasn't sure what to do. Should I reach out for her, or just let her follow? I chose the latter. She had obviously been through something traumatic and I didn't want to scare her. I took a few tentative steps and we moved inland with Zero picking up the rear, snorting like he was all kinds of proud of himself.

I heard her crying again and stopped just before we reached the clearing. Turning to face her, I saw something in her eyes. Not sure if it was panic or shock, I paused.

"My friend..."

That was the last thing she said before crumpling to the ground.

2

We were about a hundred feet from my house when she fell. I knelt in the mud beside her, felt for a pulse and then, laying her on her back, checked her more thoroughly. I put my hand in front of her face and felt her warm breath, a little uneven, but strong. She was showing signs of hyporthermia, dehydration and exhaustion, I decided she would be better off inside.

Placing her over my shoulder in a fireman's carry, I hurried back toward my house, hauling her up the back stairs to my porch. She was lighter than I'd expected and I set her gently on one of the chaise lounges. Turning on the lights, I once again checked her pulse and breath. Leaning forward, I gently squeezed her between her neck and shoulders. Her eyes opened and she coughed. I studied her and noticed some fresh bruises on her face and neck.

She was clearly alive and her condition didn't appear to be life threatening. Over the years, I've had a fair amount of training in first aid and CPR, not to the level of an EMT, but I felt my original prognosis was accurate.

Living seven miles from the mainland made me look at some of the services most people took for granted in a different light. 911 was one of them. It would take a long time to get a boat out here with qualified EMTs and equipment. I decided, against this, ignoring the constant reinforcement from the NPS lawyers that every incident, regardless of how minor, needed emergency personnel to be called. There was no need to waste resources in this case. Provided I was right about her condition, Martinez would approve of my budget conscious decision.

Fortunately, when I got back with the blood pressure cuff, her eyes were open. I could see them follow me as I approached and wondered what she remembered of our encounter.

"Water," she said.

I nodded and went inside. Returning with a glass, I handed it to her, relieved when she was able to sit upright and drink.

"Thanks," she said, draining it.

She was shivering and I went in to get her a refill and a blanket. My phone was on the counter and I thought about calling this in just in case. When I saw her standing in the door, I decided to wait. She appeared freaked out enough and I wanted some answers.

"Misty," I started, trying to gauge whether she remembered our conversation. Her last line about her friend had not been far from my mind.

She nodded. "I think you told me your name, but I don't remember."

"Kurt. Kurt Hunter," I said. "You mentioned something before you passed out about a friend?"

She looked down as if she had done something wrong.

"It's alright. I'm here to help you. I work for the National Park Service," I said, trying to reassure her.

"I lost her when we had to swim."

I'd wondered how she had gotten here. There was a channel around most of the island deep enough for a low draft boat. Someone could have dumped her, which was not likely as anyone in these waters knew there was a ranger stationed here. There was also the chance that she had fallen overboard. That seemed the most likely scenario. Though these were tropical waters, with the current temperature in the mid-seventies, even a minimal exposure, would result in signs of hypothermia. That matched her condition as well as anything, and also opened an ocean of possibilities. I realized I was still holding the blanket and handed it to her.

She entered the house, put it around her shoulders, and sat on the couch. "I don't remember much."

"What was your friend's name?" I needed something to go on. If there was another woman out there, I needed to act.

"Heather."

"And Heather was in the water with you?"

"She didn't make it."

There was no point in questioning her further. I had to do something now. Looking at the girl sitting across from me, shivering, with tears running down her cheeks, I knew I couldn't just leave her here alone. I would have to go look for her friend, but unsure of her mental state, Ray and Becky were my best option.

"I'm going to go after your friend, but first we need to go next door." She didn't respond, but got up and followed me out the door. Zero found us about halfway to their house and fell in line. We climbed the stairs to the front porch, and I knocked on the door.

It took several attempts, but finally a light came on. Becky cracked the door open.

"Come on, Zero. You live here, you know," she said, opening the door wider and looking at me. "Damned dog likes you more than me."

Zero brushed past us and into the house. "I need some help," I said, before she closed the door.

"Sure thing, hon. What can we do for ya?" Her Alabama accent sounded sleepy.

I turned to Misty. "Zero found her on the backside of the island. She says she has a friend that's missing. I need to go have a look. Can you keep her company for me?"

"Sure thing. Y'all come on in." She stepped away from the door.

I led Misty into the mirror image of my home. The only difference was this one was clearly lived in by a family. I stepped on one of Jamie's many toys strewn across the floor.

"You got a name, honey?"

"Misty," the girl said.

"I'm Becky. Let's have us a cup of tea and let Kurt go have a look for your friend," she said, leading her to the couch. "Go on, I got this," she said to me. She turned back to the girl. "That a Lilly Pulitzer you got on there? Little worse for the wear, I'll get you something dry."

I took one look at Misty and knew she was in good hands. "I'll be back soon," I said, turning and walking toward the door. Outside, I looked out at the water. The storm had passed and the weather had settled, leaving a strong north wind and clear skies. I shivered, noticing the temperature drop. There were usually several days of hot and humid weather before a front broke through, making the freshly arrived cool, dry air seem even colder.

With Misty safe, I was able to focus on the missing woman. It had crossed my mind that in Misty's condition, her girlfriend might or might not have existed, but I still had to check it out. I went across the lawn, opened the door to my house and gathered up the boat keys, my gun belt, and cell phone. On the way out, I reached for a slicker on a hook behind the door. It was lightweight, mostly useful in rain, but I hoped to add a little wind protection to the hoodie I had on.

I went down to the dock and removed the extra spring line I had attached before the storm and hopped aboard the park service issued twenty-two-foot center console. After starting the engine, I released the other lines and idled into the channel. What had once been so foreign to me was starting to come naturally, and as I let the boat drift, I calculated which direction I would expect the water to move a body. The wind was coming out of the northeast and even though we were in the lee of the landmass of Elliot Key, I would still have to factor it in. The tide was also near its peak. I had the beginning of a vague timeline estimated only by Misty's condition. At most, she had been out a few hours. That meant a flood tide and with the wind blown waves coming from the northeast, I would search to the north.

With the spotlight in one hand and the wheel in the other, I idled into the channel and started to work my way around the small island. The high tide widened the skinny channel that followed the contours of Elliot Key allowing me a little comfort level. I was being extra cautious, knowing I couldn't save anyone if I grounded. Usually this was kayak-only country. Daylight would have allowed me to gauge the depth by the colors of the water, and the depth finder was worthless, showing where I had been, not where I was going. Just to be safe, I raised the engine until the blades of the propeller just broke water. Keeping an eye on the telltale stream of water flowing from the exhaust, I moved slowly forward.

There was a chance that if the girls had come from Elliot Key, the wind would have pushed them away from the shore and the tide would have taken them counterclockwise around the island. Misty, by swimming, had shortened her path. Panning the light back and forth, I could only wonder what I was missing as the beam fought to break through the dense mangroves on the back side of Adams Key. The shallow water wouldn't allow a closer inspection and I continued, figuring I could cover much more water with the boat than if I had to go back in on foot.

It would have been nice to have gotten more information from Misty—like whether her friend was a good swimmer or under the influence of drugs or alcohol. Misty appeared to be sober when I found her, but that didn't mean she had gone into the water that way.

Even in her current condition, Misty was well dressed and though dirty, well-groomed. I had plenty of experience with meth users and other hard drugs back in the Plumas Forest, and Misty showed no signs of either. She looked like someone who took care of herself. I didn't know what a Lilly Pulitzer was, but her dress looked expensive. I could only assume her missing friend was from the same stock.

I felt the wind increase when I reached the northern end of the island and looked out at the small white-capped waves marching toward me across the open water of the bay. From here I could see Elliot Key to the right. The shore of the low island was outlined by the moon, but the interior remained dark. The lights from the campground and small harbor toward the northern end of the key were blocked by Billy's Point. The night air was clear enough that, across the water to the northwest, I could see the Miami skyline. But there was still no body.

I was fascinated by water and what it could reveal. Sometimes it had to be cajoled, and others it was in your face. Fishing was my way to learn it. I had discovered the pot grow out west by watching the water and finding an eddy with a current running the wrong way. When I tossed my fly toward it, the feather had disappeared into an irrigation pipe. It was a simple matter of tracing it from there, up the steep bank, and walking into a forest of marijuana.

This time what the water told me was clear. Heather, the missing women, would not be found north of here. The incoming tide, a weaker one this evening, couldn't combat the wind and waves that would move anything on the surface to the south.

That revelation took me around the island in the direction of the deeper channel. Before I reached it, there was a small cove with very shallow water. Even just slightly on the downside of high tide, I could see the tips of the seagrass poking through the water. It looked like there was some debris piled up on the shore and I picked my way across the shallows, shining the light at the shoreline.

Crab buoys, pallets, and all sorts of trash often floated into the mangroves— especially after a storm. It looked like more of the same until an odd shape appeared, something larger than your typical flotsam. Shining the light at it, I tried to imagine the shape of a body there—but it was too far away.

Nudging the throttle, I powered through the seagrass. I knew it was bad for the ecosystem and had often scolded boaters for the channels their propellers made—usually before grounding. The possibility of locating a body made the decision for me, and I plowed ahead until I felt the bow hit bottom. Dropping the engine to neutral, I went forward with the light getting as close to the shore as possible.

The figure was clearer now and I thought I saw the head of a woman, but it could easily have been a crab buoy from this distance. The only way to find out was to get closer. I hit the switch for the LED lights mounted below the boat and scanned the bottom. I had hoped for sand, it was the only chance I had to reach the beach. The dark seagrass waving in the current only confirmed what I had first thought—muck—a combination of ingredients that were more like quicksand than mud. With this type of bottom and stuck almost fifty yards away, wading to shore was off the table. I had tried that once only to sink almost to my hips in the dark muck below the grass.

The only way was in the kayak or on foot. In either case, I needed to get back to the dock. The engine kicked in protest when I dropped it into reverse and started to back out of the shallow water. Just as I reached deep water, I heard the sound of another boat. It startled me at first after hearing nothing but my own engine and the wind for the past half hour. It was unusual for someone to be out so soon after a storm.

3

THE WIND CARRIED THE SOUND OF THE ENGINE ACROSS THE WATER making it appear closer than it was. Had it been blowing the other way, I probably wouldn't have heard it at all. A quick scan of the horizon showed nothing.

I heard the boat again and instinctively turned. I saw what I thought was a shadow, but after staring at it for a moment saw the silhouette of a boat. Just as I saw it, the navigation lights, which I swore had been off, flickered on. It was suspicious behavior and had they remained off, it would have been cause to check them out. What would have been an easy excuse to take a look at the boat was gone. I might have checked it out anyway, but it was possible that the girl's body was on the beach. Pulling the handheld spotlight from its holder, I spun the boat and faced the shore. Panning the beam across the beach, I wondered once again if it was her. The figure was still there and had to be my first priority.

I made my decision based on doing the right thing. More often than not, this put Martinez and me at odds. This time he would agree. My mandate from him was clear: if there was no apparent wrongdoing, move along. The park service was notoriously underfunded and one of the first things shut down when Congress failed to pass a budget. We all knew it was posturing, but when the notices said to go home, there was no choice. Our shortcomings often fell to Miami-Dade and several other alphabet agencies, who often assisted us—reluctantly. The FDLE, Florida Department of Law Enforcement, was often helpful, but the closest office was in Tampa. FWC, the Florida Fish and Wildlife Commission and ICE both had boats stationed on the bay out of the same marina as our headquarters. I had contacts in both, but had to use them carefully.

As I spun the wheel and turned toward open water, I studied the boat. It appeared to be cruising at about six knots and staying to the channel. There was nothing to indicate that they were fishing either, which eliminated Pete Robinson and the FWC. I thought about giving Johnny Wells, my buddy from ICE, a call to see if he'd take a look. If he weren't already out on patrol, the boat would be gone before he got here.

I was back at the dock in minutes. It was a noisy landing and I heard Zero coming after me. Brushing him aside, I went for the kayak leaning against the house. With the plastic shell dragging behind me and the paddle in hand, I reached the dock and shoved the boat into the water. I had learned a few tricks, mostly from the mistakes I had made since I had been here and always kept a line tied to the bow of the kayak which I used to reel it back to the dock. Climbing down the ladder, I found my balance in the small boat and pushed away from the piling.

Not having to worry about grounding now, I hugged the shoreline, which allowed me to stay out of the wind and reached the small beach in less time than it took to motor there in the larger boat. Shining my mag light on the shore, I blinked hard and followed the beam. There was nothing on the beach that remotely resembled the figure I had seen from the boat. Confused, I looked around and noticed the lights from the larger boat I had seen earlier receding into the distance. There was something suspicious about the boat. If I had the center console, I could have followed them, but in the kayak, with the wind blowing in my face, I'd be lucky to paddle at two or three mph. The phosphorescence from the boat told me they were up on plane and running at about twenty.

I had been in law enforcement for a dozen years now and knew there were no such things as coincidences. Misty's statement about a lost friend convinced me the figure I'd seen on the beach was her. The larger boat was no coincidence either. Putting that aside, I beached the kayak and pulled it above the tideline. With the light in my left hand and my gun in my right, I started into the mangroves. Wishing I had brought better footwear, I skidded and tripped on the invisible roots and debris. Pointing the light at the ground might have saved my bare feet but would do nothing to help find the girl.

The island was small enough that I crossed it in a few minutes. Finding nothing of interest, I turned back and started a search pattern. After thirty minutes, my feet were shredded and I had found nothing. Back at the beach, I took my time inspecting the shoreline thinking I might have been wrong and was chasing a figment from Misty's mind. After my short time with her, I started thinking this was the case. Although there were no blatant signs of the hard stuff I was used to, I suspected drugs or alcohol were involved. Most of my experience had been in dealing with pot and meth; these girls would probably fall into the designer drug category.

I stood there, looking out across the water and tried to place myself back in my boat, so I could imagine where on the beach I had seen the figure. Thinking it had been about twenty feet to my right, slowly and deliberately, I walked in that direction. At a pace slow enough that I was able to see the smaller trash brought in by the tide, I moved toward the spot, but there was no body. I was about to turn around, write this whole adventure off to craziness, and leave Misty in the custody of Miami-Dade when I saw the footprint.

It was a beach only in the sense that there was a small flat area with no mangroves intruding on it. There was no white sand. Mostly it was covered in debris: leaves, twigs, and seagrass brought in by the tide. There were few clear areas, but I had been more focused on the brush on my first pass. Now, with the light shining at the ground, I saw the indentation of a boat shoe in the sand. It was well defined and below the high tide line. It had been placed here in the last few hours.

Misty had been barefoot, so unless she had lost her shoes, it wasn't hers. Leaning over to inspect it, I guessed it belonged to a man. I was no forensics expert. Justine could probably judge the height and weight of the person by the depth of the print. To me, it simply looked too large for a woman. I hovered my bare foot over it for reference and knew I was correct. The print was larger than my foot. Finding the first clue that I wasn't crazy set me on a thorough search of the mangroves. Perspective is everything and once I was sure that the body was gone, I took my time. After retrieving several pieces of torn clothing from a branch that I thought might have blood on it, I returned to the kayak and placed the evidence on the seat.

The footprint was a big clue and with the tide coming in now, there was no time to do the usual documentation. Forget about a tape measure, I didn't even have my phone to take a picture of it. Justine and Martinez would probably have the same reaction to what I was about to do, but I had no choice. I removed the plastic cover from the water-tight compartment on the kayak and brought it to the footprint. Using the hard, plastic edge, I dug as deep as I could and slid the cover underneath the indentation. The sand started to fall apart as I went. All I could do was hope that I could remove it and get it back to my house without destroying it. The other evidence might have been proof that Misty was right. This could prove foul play and provide a valuable clue.

With what was left of the print on the lid, I returned to the kayak and set it on the beach. I placed the other evidence inside the compartment and looked for a place to hold the cover. The exterior of the kayak had bungee cord systems in both the bow and stern, but using them would crush the delicate sand. The only choice was my lap. Placing the lid on the seat, I pulled the kayak into the water. Before I started to sink into the muck, I straddled the seat—removing the lid before I sat. It fit on my lap and, using exaggerated strokes so as not to disturb it, I paddled back to the dock.

Once there I encountered another problem. Built for larger boats and the occasional storm surge, the concrete surface was several feet above my head. Under the best of circumstances, with little wind and a high tide, it was a circus act to reach the dock without going for a swim. Now with the lid on my lap, I was stuck. I sat there for several minutes trying to figure out what to do when I noticed the light was still on in Ray and Becky's house. My best option was the island's alarm and I called out to Zero.

It didn't take long before I heard the screen door open and the sound of small toenails on the concrete dock. Unfamiliar with me sitting in the kayak, he started to bark. I let him go until finally, the door opened again and I heard Ray trying to calm him down. I urged him on and finally, Ray, with no other choice, investigated. He stood above me with Zero by his side.

"Sorry for the bother, but I could use a little help."

"Bothering's been going on since you brought that girl over. Becky's been fussing with her since you left. Now, the damned dog's woken Jamie."

I knew Ray liked his routines, and one of those were regular hours. Island time was best lived by the sun and tides. After a few weeks out here I had acclimated to it as well. "Can you take this?" There was no point in apologizing any further. He was a man of action, not words.

"What you got there?" he leaned over to look at the lid.

"Evidence. Misty said there was another girl. I didn't find her, but I did find this."

"Humph. Don't know what you're going to get out of a broken-up footprint."

I wasn't sure either, but I extended my arms until he took it. Once it was safely on the dock, I pulled myself to the ladder and climbed to the surface. Smelling the muck around my ankles, Zero came right for me. "I better hose off, and then I'll take that girl off your hands."

"That'd be a good thing. Becky gets a little lonely out here. She's probably interviewing her to be a babysitter right now." He shook his head, called Zero, and walked back to the house.

I figured Becky was going to be upset, but I had to get Misty to the mainland and figure out what was going on. Following Ray and Zero, I stopped at an intersection where the path branched off to the day-use area and using the wash station there, cleaned my feet. My toenails still reflected my adventure, but with the rest of me fairly clean, I went toward the house.

I called out through the screen door, and figuring Ray had left it open for me to retrieve what was mine, walked in. Becky and Misty sat at the kitchen table drinking tea and chatting like old friends. Misty was loosely outfitted in some of Becky's old clothes and had cleaned up her hair and face. Makeup attempted to cover the bruises, but they were still evident.

"We gotta go," I said. "I found some evidence of your friend across the island, but I think someone has taken her. "

"Becky said I could stay here," Misty said, looking over at Becky for support.

"Girl needs a friend, Kurt." Becky folded her arms over her chest.

"I'll bring her back if you both like, but for now, I have to take her to Miami-Dade to give a statement."

"No," Misty said, matching Becky's posture and looking at her.

"What do you mean, no?" I asked.

Becky eyed me. I had seen that look before and knew I was in trouble. I only hoped Misty and her friend were in less trouble than me.

4

"What do you mean no?" I repeated and motioned Becky to the side.

"That girl's been through enough for one night," Becky pleaded.

"Her friend's out there. I saw her and now she's gone." I said it before I realized how badly it sounded. Ray, who had moved closer to us, tried to save me.

"You got to let him do his job. "

"No reason he can't do his job with the girl safe and sound here," Becky said.

She was an immovable force. Ray and I looked at each other and shrugged. "I need a few minutes alone with her to take her statement," I told her.

"Don't you make that girl cry," Becky warned.

With a truce in place, Becky went over to the table and whispered something to Misty. I could tell she didn't like it, but after a few more words of reassurance, she got up and came toward me. I looked at her as if for the first time. She looked entirely different from the girl I had found only a few hours ago. Her body language told me that she was good with men. Her movements were subtle and well-practiced, maybe even coached. She was pretty, in a teenage innocent sort of way, and I pinned her for a hair flipper. Even with Becky's clothing hanging lose on her frame, I could tell she had a good body.

She came toward me with a confidence that was confusing considering everything that she had been through tonight. I got the feeling that, law enforcement agent or not, she was used to getting her way with men. Where many men would have been attracted by her and subconsciously acted differently, she wasn't my type. I preferred my women to be my contemporaries, not their children.

"Why don't you sit down," I motioned to the couch and sat in an adjacent chair. Questions were already formed in my mind, and I took a deep breath before starting. Her facade might have exuded confidence, but I could see how scared she was by her eyes. She probably used them to seduce, but I was a trained investigator and looked past their hazel beauty and saw the truth. I would have to be careful or she would shut down. Reaching for my notepad, I found only the empty pockets of my cargo pants. Motioning to Becky like I was writing something down, she gave me a look that warned me to be careful—that she was watching—and brought me a pad and pen.

"Let's start with basics, okay?" I asked.

"Sure."

"Your name and date of birth would be a good start."

"Misty Melody," she said. "I'm nineteen."

In one sentence, I had learned that her name was not Misty and she wasn't nineteen. I had to tread more carefully now, especially if she was underage. Despite the fact that I was sure the response was fabricated, I wrote down her answers. I'd circle back and try to get the truth later. "Where are you from?"

"I'm from Tampa."

I wrote that down too. It was probably correct. Experienced liars stayed as close to the truth as possible. "What brings you to Miami?"

"Me and my friend Heather, we got a job offer here."

"What kind of work were you doing?" I kind of knew the answer already.

"We're hostesses."

She said it proudly. Looking over at Becky, I wondered if she was able to hear our conversation. It had reached the point that I wanted a witness and asked her to come over. Once she was seated, I started to dig a little harder. "What does a hostess do?" I hoped she was going to say seat people in a restaurant, but knew that was not going to be the answer.

"We make our guests comfortable," she said, looking at Becky.

I saw the scared little girl coming out and backed off. "Can we call any family to help you out?"

That got me a look I should have expected. Becky saved me.

"We're here for you, sweetheart."

Misty looked relieved.

"Does your friend," I paused to look at my notes, "Heather. Does she have a last name?" I asked.

"Flowers," Misty said.

She clearly knew that I knew it wasn't the truth, and she looked at Becky for reassurance. I wasn't sure if Becky understood what was going on here. If she did, she wasn't showing any signs and was giving reassurance where needed.

"Where do you guys live?"

"Like an address?"

It took everything I had to keep the look out of my eyes and the tone from my voice. My daughter, Allie was almost fifteen now. I knew a little about teenage girls. Fortunately, she continued.

"We live on boats," she said.

The boat I had seen earlier came to mind. "I saw a boat while I was looking for Heather, was that where you were before I found you?"

"Maybe, I don't know what boat you saw. We were out on a job."

I would have loved to hear what that entailed, but caught a warning from Becky. "Do you remember the name of the boat you were on?"

"*Temptress*. We went out of the marina by South Beach."

Finally, I had something that might be helpful. "What about the boat you live on?"

"*Spindrift*."

"What marina is *Spindrift* in?" I asked.

"We just move around. Last place was up in Boca."

I would have preferred her residence to have a number and street name. Misty made a display of yawning. Whether she did it on purpose or not, I was uncomfortably aware of her body as she raised her arms over her head. There was no time to turn away.

"I think that's enough for right now. Maybe you can finish in the morning," Becky said.

My eyes caught Ray's. We were from different worlds, but both knew the look on Becky's face. This was not open for discussion. "I've got a good place to start," I said, rising from the chair. I said my goodbyes, offering Ray a look that said I felt his pain. He nodded back.

"Come back in the morning," he said and locked the door behind me.

I knew that he wanted Misty out of there as soon as possible and I didn't blame him. I walked to the intersection where the path split; one side going to the dock, and the other to my house. There was no way sleep was coming, and looking at my watch, I saw it was almost midnight. Justine worked until two and I wanted access to her crime lab—and seeing her was always a bonus. I quickly changed clothes, gathered the evidence I had collected, and sent her a text that I had a missing person. It probably wasn't going to get the same excited response I could expect if I had a dead body, but it worked.

The front had passed, leaving a steady northeast breeze making my trip back to headquarters a little bumpy. With the wind at my back, the ride was at least dry and I made it to the dock in forty minutes. After pulling into my slip, I tied the boat off, using an extra spring line to keep the wind from pushing the port side into the adjacent piling, and then walked to the parking lot. Passing the front of the building, I couldn't help but look up, half expecting a light on in Martinez's office. I knew my boss tracked my movements and if there was something going on, I suspected he had some kind of alarm that told him I was at it again. The window was dark and I thought that maybe a pre-emptive strike would be a good idea, and decided to send him an email detailing what had happened as soon as I reached the crime lab.

Susan McLeash's office was also dark. After seeing her leading a tour group a few weeks ago, I wondered if it was still hers. My counterpart and partner, when Martinez could force her on me, had already been on probation for killing a suspect in one of my cases last summer. She had followed that up by discharging my weapon at a protest and then using my rifle in the Turkey Point case. At Martinez's urging, I had covered up the first incident, but there were Miami-Dade officers present at the latter. I had done my best to protect her in my report, but anyone reading between the lines would know what she had done. Now, I expected the worst she could do to me was toss me a dirty look whenever she saw me—I only hoped that was the case.

I reached my park service truck, newly repaired from my last off-road experience. Of course, with the feds footing the bill, the work was flawless. I could only wonder about the park service's priorities. I wasn't sure if it was Martinez or someone higher up that made the decision, but spending the money up front for four-wheel drive would have been cheaper than the subsequent repairs. While I drove the deserted streets through Homestead to the Turnpike, I wondered how I was going to survive the personalities and bureaucracy of the park. At least in the Plumas National Forest, where I had been stationed before, I had ten thousand acres to patrol alone. My closest boss was an hour away. South Florida often felt like an alternate universe.

There was no traffic on the turnpike and I let my brain change directions to Misty and her friend. I wondered where she was from and how her parents had raised her to turn into a "hostess". I had heard long ago that one of the primary goals of a father was to keep his daughter off the pole. I guessed her father had failed her.

The parking lot of the Miami-Dade Crime Lab was also deserted. I hoped that meant Justine had experienced a slow night and could help me. Walking downstairs, my mood instantly improved when I saw her through the glass partition in the hallway. Justine stood with her back to me, swaying to the music I knew was loudly pumping through her headphones. Her tight braid moved behind her, alternating between hitting each well-developed shoulder. As a standup paddleboard racer, she liked the night shift because it allowed her to train almost every day. She did well in her races, but I preferred the other benefits of her training as I watched her body sway beneath the lab coat.

Before I was done admiring her, she must have sensed me standing there and turned around. With a smile, she invited me in. I entered and gave her a peck on the cheek, our agreed-on work greeting. Fraternization was discouraged, but we worked for different entities and though some frowned on it, we had made peace with it.

"I'm very disappointed she's alive," she said, then smacked my arm.

"Yeah, I know. Sad isn't it." I asked her the question that had been on my mind since the interview. "How do good girls go bad?" I knew it was a mistake to say as soon as it came out of my mouth.

"Are you getting involved with another victim. It was alright with Abbey, but what's up now?"

I decided to leave it there and move on. Abbey had been my first real case, at least my first victim with a name. "Got one live one and one missing one—maybe dead." It was interesting how immune I had gotten to death in the last few months.

"And the game begins."

5

I had her attention now. "How busy are you? I have some evidence I'd like you to look at." Her brow furrowed and her smile was gone. I wondered if I'd blown it again by bringing too much work into our relationship.

"I got a talking-to about some of the extracurricular things going on."

I had noticed several packing boxes around and expected the worst. Now it was my turn to be worried. Justine had helped me on several cases. If it were not for her taking down Dwayne, a crooked detective involved in a human smuggling ring, I would be dead. Without her, there would likely be a handful of additional dead bodies. "I'm so sorry. I never intended for you to get in trouble."

"It was just a verbal reprimand. No paperwork. I just have to watch myself and get approval before going off the reservation again."

She must have noticed me checking out the boxes.

"They're moving me upstairs to the new lab. Kind of a bummer, really. Like moving back in with your parents."

I knew she had resisted the change, liking the privacy of the lower level better than the newly remodeled, high-tech facility. I had to think quickly. There was a missing girl out there and I needed

Justine's help to find her. "What if I filed a report with Miami-Dade?"

She thought for a minute. "That would work for a start. This time of night there's no one to call for approval and as long as you have a case number, I can allocate my hours."

After paying for the new lab, the Miami-Dade bureaucracy had extended its tentacles into the forensics business. There was now an administrator in charge—instead of the head technician. I had some first-hand experience with bosses like that. Martinez did everything by the book—except occasionally cutting Susan McLeash some slack in exchange for undocumented favors. Otherwise, it was all about the budget. My own ethos was to act now and ask for forgiveness later. Sometimes it worked; others it didn't, and that was a risk I was happy to take. I didn't want to extend that to Justine.

"I'll go call it in." I turned away.

"Maybe you should call your friend Grace," she said.

I couldn't read her tone. Grace Herrera was a detective with Miami-Dade. She was extremely attractive, but had never been anything but professional. Before I could weigh the pros and cons, she explained herself.

"Really. She's the best we have. Making a random call to report something in this department is a crap shoot."

"Okay." I had to agree with her. "It's almost two. Maybe I should wait until morning."

"I didn't realize it was that late. It's been a slow night. I'll clock out and have a look on my own time. If it pans out, I'll document my hours later. But, make sure you call her in the morning."

I breathed a sigh of relief. Hopefully, before Martinez could reach his twin monitors sitting to the side of his desk and figure out what I had been up to all night, I would be well on my way to a solution. "I've got the evidence in the truck."

"We should probably backdoor-it, just in case. I'll meet you where the van is parked."

I left the lab and went upstairs. There was no one behind the desk so I escaped unobserved. I walked to my truck and looked over at the footprint sitting in the passenger seat. It had eroded in the last half hour and I had my doubts what Justine could do with it. Just in case it got worse, I took a picture with my phone. There was no activity in the lot so I drove around to the side of the building and parked next to the crime scene van. Justine was by the door and motioned for me. I got out and walked around to the passenger door with what was left of the footprint. Opening it, I reached over to grab the hatch. As careful as I was, the movement caused the already decayed heal section to crumble.

"You have to keep them wet until you can cast them," Justine said and took the hatch cover like a mother taking back her baby.

I went back to the truck for the pieces of clothing and the branch with what I thought was blood. She had propped the door open and was already in the lab, hovering over the footprint, when I entered. There was a sense of urgency in her movements and I chose to stand back and let her do her thing.

From where I stood, I watched her spray the footprint with an aerosol can. The dirt immediately darkened and after about a minute, it looked like it had hardened.

"You can breathe now. I think I've got what's left of it."

I moved closer, staying an arm's length away, not wanting to do any more damage than I had already done. Even under the bright lights, the tread of the shoe barely showed . It might not be good enough for a trial, but from the pattern, I confirmed my guess that it was a boat shoe. My mind went back to the two boat names Misty had given me and I took out my notepad. "Can we access the Miami-Dade tax assessor's site? The girl I found gave me a couple of boat names that I want to run. I think whoever left this came off of one of them."

"You needing my super-secret password?"

"That's what I'm here for." I gave her bottom a pat, and walked to the computer station.

After logging onto the site, I entered the names, starting with the *Temptress*. Half a dozen entries appeared on the screen. "Wow." I tried *Spindrift* next and got only four. I wrote down the information in my notepad and looked at Justine. It was past three, and the adrenaline that had gotten me through the last few hours, after finding Misty and looking for her friend, had worn off.

"You look beat. Maybe we should get you a few hours of sleep," Justine said.

Though I didn't want to admit it, I knew she was right. Slowing down often got better results than my first instinct of barreling through a case until it was solved. As it turned out, sleep was everything my grandmother said it was. "Okay, I don't think I can get anything else done before morning." Knowing that dawn was only a few hours away helped a little and I promised myself that I'd give Grace an early wake-up call.

I followed Justine back to her apartment and waited for her to open the door. She'd recently given me a key and we had quickly moved past that to shared passwords for our phones—a level-five relationship. Minutes later, we were under the covers and the idea of sleep was gone.

My internal clock was usually dependable, but I had learned to set an alarm when I stayed at Justine's. Her blackout shades eliminated any trace of the sun and I had been awakened here by Martinez more times than I wanted to count. There were better ways to wake up, and when the alarm on my phone went off, I rolled over only to find the bed empty.

"See ya, sunshine," Justine called on her way out the door.

She was dressed to paddle. Besides dead bodies, racing stand-up paddleboards was her passion. In order to get her miles in she needed to get an early start—before the boaters were out and the sea breeze kicked in. She often woke at dawn to paddle and took a nap in the afternoon before work. I rolled out of bed and looked at my phone—it was seven. I took a quick shower to buy Grace a few more minutes of sleep, and when I was ready, sat down at the kitchen table with a cup of coffee. With my notepad in front of me, I pulled up her contact information, and pressed the phone icon.

While I waited, I started composing an email to Martinez in my head. Her phone rang three times before a sleepy voice answered. I paused, feeling guilty for waking her, but knew there was no getting out of it. My name was probably staring at her on the phone's display. Grace saved me from an awkward opening when she answered.

"Well, Special Agent Hunter, what can Miami-Dade do for the NPS?"

As a trained agent, I detected a slight tinge of sarcasm in her tone. That was a good thing. Grace was always professional and I was glad she made the first step by opening up. "Sorry if I woke you. Got a missing person that I thought maybe you could help with."

"My case or yours?"

Our jurisdictions were clear, but the lines were sometimes blurry. Anything that happened within the park's boundaries was mine; what happened outside of them was hers. The problem was that the bad guys didn't always stay within the lines. We had worked well together before. Unlike our superiors, neither of us were out for accolades or commendations. I'm not into all the spiritual stuff, but there is a verse from the Tao that I remembered about being humble and praise will find you:

When the Master governs, the people are hardly aware that he exists.
Next best is a leader who is loved.
Next, one who is feared.
The worst is one who is despised.

That last was clearly Martinez.

"I found a girl in the park last night. She says she had a friend with her, who is now missing."

"Now?"

"It's complicated. Can you help me file a report? I guess there's new orders from the Ivory Tower that you guys can't help me without a case number."

"I got that memo, too. I can meet you in an hour."

She gave me the name of a coffee shop. I thanked her and wondered why I had that tingling feeling you get when a pretty girl says yes to a date. On my way to our rendezvous, I wondered why we weren't meeting at her office. I guessed there was a pretty good chance I'd become a persona non grata with Miami-Dade.

I parked and, with butterflies in my stomach, approached the coffee shop. I relaxed when I saw her sitting alone near the corner. She greeted me like an old friend. There was no awkwardness or glances around to see if anyone was looking.

"I like to work here," she said as if reading my mind.

"Cool, can I get you anything?"

"Sure."

She gave me her drink order, which I had to repeat back three times. Finally she told me to tell the barista it was for her and they would know. I don't know why, but I expected the typical LEO drink —black coffee—and wondered if this wasn't one of the reasons why she worked from here. While the barista made her drink and poured my black coffee, I thought about how to present this.

"So, you saw a body and when you returned, it wasn't there?"

I had decided to tell her the unvarnished truth. "Yeah. I couldn't get in there with the park service boat. It was less than a half hour between when I saw what I believed to be the body and when I returned."

She was quiet for a few minutes while she wrote down the sequence of events. "The boat names that you were given?"

"*Temptress* and *Spindrift*."

She wrote those down as well. "Any kind of description on the boat you actually saw would help. I'm thinking that the girls are your deal. I can help you track down the boats."

I shut my eyes and tried to picture the boat I'd seen in my mind. I couldn't remember anything but a vague outline highlighted by the moon. Then I remembered the navigation lights. I had learned a few things about boats in my time here and one of them was how to recognize a particular boat by the configuration of its lights. Sailboats were easy—a white anchor light was set on top of the mast. Smaller outboards generally had a lower anchor light and a common green and red beacon mounted to the bow. Generally, the height of the vessel could be determined by the white light and its beam, or width, by the distance between its red and green lights.

From what I recalled, the boat had separate port and starboard lights. The anchor light had been the height of a flybridge. I drew Grace a picture and together we filled in the gaps. It looked like a trawler, a motorboat used mainly by live-aboards and partiers.

With the report finished, we had an awkward moment where neither of us knew what to say next. It ended quickly when my phone vibrated on the table. I looked down and saw that it was Martinez.

6

THE TIME ON MY PHONE'S DISPLAY SHOWED IT WAS AFTER NINE. I KNEW his hours and realized I had forgotten to send him an email. I should have at least called him before I met with Grace. Pointing at the phone, I made a face and stepped to the side.

"What the hell, Hunter," he started, obviously knowing I was in Miami and not on the bay.

I pictured him sitting in front of his dual monitors watching a little blinking light that told him my whereabouts. "Had to file a report with Miami-Dade. There was some action last night."

"You file your reports with me before you go running to your girlfriend's up there."

Aside from the girlfriend comment, he was probably right. I would regret not sending him that email. I could only hope that finding Misty and her missing friend late at night might give me some quarter. "I'll be down to explain." I had learned long ago that bad news was better delivered in person. And in Martinez's world, this was bad news.

"I'll be here," he said and disconnected.

Where else would he be at this time of day? Later, it might be a good question. Usually after a late lunch, he disappeared. I turned back to Grace. "I gotta go. Can you keep me posted on any progress?"

"You bet, and good luck with your boss. He's a piece of work."

I was already standing and she remained seated when I thanked her and said goodbye. The table provided a comfortable barrier between us. With Grace working on the two boats and Justine's promise to look at the rest of the evidence once I got a case number, which I texted to her, my next course of action was to appease Martinez and get Misty off my island.

I almost wished I was stuck in the rush-hour traffic heading northbound on the Turnpike toward Miami. The continuing construction in the southbound lanes slowed me a little yet most of the ride was at the speed limit—as if the traffic gods were rushing me toward my meeting with Martinez. Despite solving the last two cases and giving him his coveted podium several times in the last few months, he still had me on a short leash. The budget was his war cry. I couldn't have cared less, I'm not a numbers guy.

On my way into the office I saw Mariposa sitting at the reception desk. The matronly Jamaican was my only real ally here so I went over to say hello. We chatted for a minute and she extended another invitation to dinner and that special rum her husband was only allowed to drink with guests. I guessed that either Justine and I had passed the audition, or the Appleton 21 was good enough that her husband didn't care who he drank with. She gave me a warm smile when I promised to ask Justine, and then a warning that Martinez had already asked twice if I had arrived. I walked upstairs, past Susan's closed office and through the open door of Martinez's lair.

He was on the phone, as he always seemed to be when I arrived. Raising a finger, he pointed toward the chair across from his desk and continued with his urgent business. While I waited, I tried to get a look at his dual surveillance monitors, but he had carefully positioned the visitor's chair so I could only see the sides. Finally, he hung up.

"Damned bureaucrats," he complained. "Now they want revised budgets in case our funding gets cut."

I would have liked to point out that with Susan assigned to do tours—I was on my own. Our budget had been halved at my expense. "They'll figure it out. It's all posturing."

"I hope so. Can't afford to be furloughed."

I'd had enough of the pleasantries. "I found a girl on Adams Key last night. She was a mess, and said she had a friend who was missing." I quickly explained my search and the need to file a report with Miami-Dade. "I didn't want to wake you."

"Filing the report was the right action. Just get me in the loop earlier. Email works."

I'd have to remember that tip. "We've got two boat names from the girl that detective Herrera is working on and the crime lab has some evidence I collected." He didn't ask where Misty was, and I didn't tell him.

"If either of the boats picked up the missing girl, it's likely out of the park. Maybe you should do a patrol around the northern end where it was headed and make sure."

That made sense. I might get lucky and find it, and he might get lucky if it was gone and the case got passed to Miami-Dade. Leaving on peaceful terms was the best I could expect and I took it. "I'll email you with whatever I find."

He nodded, picked up the phone as if he had some more urgent business and dismissed me. I took what I thought was a win and headed downstairs, waving to Mariposa as I left. On the way to my slip, I passed Susan's boat, tied up as usual for a hurricane. I stepped aboard my twenty-two-foot center console, started the engine and went to remove the lines. Slowly I backed out of the slip. After clearing the piling, I headed out of the channel.

The marina by Bayfront Park was to the right and I decided to make a quick pass. Misty had said the *Spindrift* had last docked up in Boca, a little over two hours away, but boats moved. There was always the chance that it or the *Temptress* was there. It was a small marina by Miami standards, and it only took a few minutes to cruise through it. There were no boats with those names and I turned to head out of the channel toward open water when I saw Chico at the ramp pulling his flat boat onto his trailer.

"Water's starting to heat up. You might get that bone bite toward the end of the week," he called to me.

I waved a thanks and continued out of the channel. Chico was one of the guides who had helped me learn to fish the waters here. Many of the other guides stayed to themselves, but I had made friends with some, more for their eyes than advice. Men like Chico were on the water every day. With the limited resources of the park service, they were a valuable tool.

Misty's whereabouts hadn't come up in my conversation with Martinez. It wasn't a failure to disclose on my part, I put the onus on him to ask. Before heading out to patrol the northern end of the park, I decided to take a quick run by Adams Key, hoping I could pry Misty away from Becky's protective grasp and give Grace a turn at her. I figured she would respond better to a female than to me.

The wind was still blowing from the northeast and had a cold bite to it. It also caused me to slow down and halve the speed I usually cruised at. The park service bay boat had a low freeboard and shallow draft. It was great for patrolling the park, but delivered a wet ride in choppy water. Forty-five minutes later, I was tied up at the long concrete dock running parallel to Adams Key. Ray's boat was there, a rare occurrence during the day. There were also two pleasure boats tied up near the end by the day-use area.

It was also strange that there was no sign of Zero. I tied off the lines and hopped onto the dock wondering what was going on. I didn't have long to wait. The screen door slammed and Ray emerged. Zero was at his heels, running toward me.

"Hey. You got a plan for that girl?" Ray asked.

Zero parked himself between us and I reached down and petted him. "I'd like to get her to the detective at Miami-Dade."

"Anything to get her out of here."

"What's up?" I knew Becky was often lonely, having only a three-year-old and Zero to keep her company while Ray was off keeping the out islands running.

"Caught her with Becky's phone and now she's threatening this, that, and the other thing. Damned girl's trouble."

"Did she take anything?"

"Just the phone, but she needs to be gone before anything else happens."

I nodded and followed him toward the house. As we neared the door, I could hear the two women arguing. Becky came out of the house with Jamie slung over her shoulder like a bag of flour. She slammed the door behind her.

"You got to take her, Kurt. Girl's a handful of trouble."

"No problem. I was wanting to get her to Miami-Dade to talk to a detective there anyway." I wasn't sure what was going on here, but if Becky and Ray were done with her it would make things easier for me. I lived out here, too, and that made it three to one that she had to go. I wasn't sure where Zero stood, and Jamie was too young to vote. "Let's go talk to her."

"I'll wait out here," Becky said, moving closer to Ray.

He placed an arm around her. I shrugged and turned toward the door. Opening it, I saw Misty with the phone in one hand and a knife in the other. "Can we sit down and talk?"

"I've got nothing to talk about," she sobbed, and made a threatening move with the knife. It wasn't my first rodeo with a crazed knife-wielding person and I could tell from the way she gripped it with the blade facing down that she didn't know how to use it.

I lunged forward and grabbed the hand that held the knife. I wasn't sure if it was just more drama or a serious attempt, but I knew she needed more help than she could get here. When she tried to pull away, I twisted her wrist, applying as little pressure as possible until she released the knife. It dropped to the floor and she backed to the counter. We stood, staring at each other. "There's a woman with Miami-Dade I'd like you to talk to," I said, hoping that would at least get her to the mainland.

"Anything to get me out of here."

I guess my idea of paradise was not hers. There wasn't much need for hostesses out here. "Okay. Let's take a ride."

I was positive the knife act was drama. She had probably had enough of family life and wanted out, but just in case, I let her lead the way to the dock. She passed Becky, Ray, and Jamie with her head down and without a word of thanks. Even Zero stayed where he was. I heard Becky mutter a thank you to me under her breath and then they disappeared inside their house.

"Where are you taking me?" Misty asked, after we had boarded the park service boat. That was actually a good question. I had assumed Grace would want to talk to her, but I hadn't called her. Picking up my phone, I tried to figure out how to explain my situation without alarming Misty. I took the easy way out and texted her, asking that she meet us at the dock on Dodge Island. It was going to be a long, wet ride, but I didn't want Misty anywhere near headquarters or Martinez.

I released the lines and pulled away from the dock without answering. She had nowhere to go except overboard—which was probably how she got here in the first place.

7

Misty seemed to be comfortable on the boat. Her body swayed with the motion of the seas without her guiding it, something it took a while to learn. I guessed she had been on boats for a while, whether as a kid or a hostess—I didn't know. With one eye on her and another on the water ahead, I gripped the wheel tightly, having to steer each wave to avoid getting soaked. Looking over at her, I couldn't help but get the feeling she had more boating experience than I did.

The tide was running against the northwest wind, stacking up white-capped waves that barreled toward us. We were running right into it, making it hard to navigate. It was too rough to get the small boat up on plane and I had to concentrate as each wave cresting under the boat threw us off course. Throughout the hour-long beating Misty stayed in the same position, leaning against the seat rest with one hand loosely gripping the stainless-steel support for the T-top. Her face was stuck in a grimace that I guessed was not as much from the ride as her situation.

We ran past the decaying houses out at Stiltsville and finally reached the southern tip of Key Biscayne, which helped to block the weather, and the seas flattened to a light chop. I increased speed and was able to get the boat up on plane as we crossed under the Rickenbacker Causeway. Dodge Island was just ahead and I had a moment of doubt about what to do with Misty if Grace had not arrived yet. As was my habit, my gun belt was in the watertight glove box under the helm. I kept it there to keep it out of my way and protect it from the elements. I wondered if there was a way to retrieve it without causing Misty any further anxiety.

She still seemed oblivious as I pulled up to the large tires that protected the commercial dock. Even at high tide, the oversized cleats lining the concrete pier were almost out of reach. Now, at low tide, I had to take the lines and climb onto the pavement to tie off the boat. Not knowing how long I was going to be here, I secured the bow and stern as well as setting a forward and aft spring line just in case the wind turned. When I was done, I scanned the concrete expanse in front of me for Grace.

Except for the Miami Pilots' Station at the eastern tip, the man-made island was a working dock. Shipping containers were stacked in neat rows and even the cruise ship port on the other side was just a parking lot. From where we were I couldn't see past the first stack of containers. I pulled out my phone and watched Misty as I waited for Grace to answer. She was facing away from me, looking out toward South Beach. Something was familiar about her position. With her body against the seat, she rested both elbows on it and looked like she was reading a book. Except it wasn't a book—she was texting someone with Becky's phone.

I had last seen it on the counter and tried to remember if she had made a move toward it. I did recall her sliding her back against the counter but had thought nothing of it. The whole knife business must have been a ploy to distract me while she grabbed it. She must have slid it into the back pocket of Becky's jeans, which hung loosely on her slight frame. I was unsure what to do about it, besides recover the phone for Becky. Misty wasn't under arrest, or even a suspect. After taking another look at the parking lot, I jumped down to the deck of the boat.

I must have startled her, because she tried to hide the phone. I extended my hand for it. A sly look came over her face and I saw her glance at the parking lot. A vehicle was approaching and I followed her gaze. The look turned to a smile and I heard a splash. I didn't have to turn back to know that she had tossed the phone over. Becky and Ray were right. The sooner this girl was gone, the better.

"Detective Herrera should be here any minute. Why don't we go up on the dock?" I waited for her to climb up before following. She was shorter than me and had to hoist herself up. Using the tire for a foothold, she gained the concrete dock and as soon as both feet were on the ground, she took off at a run. I jumped onto the pavement and was about to go after her when I saw a white van stop and the door open. Misty ran to the passenger door, jumped in and disappeared. Tires screeched as the driver spun the van and headed through a narrow gap between two stacks of containers.

I stood there staring after them. Before I could decide what to do, a Miami-Dade cruiser pulled up.

"She's gone. A white van just grabbed her," I yelled to Grace and ran around to the passenger side. The door was locked and we lost another valuable second. The lock released and I jumped in, directing Grace toward where the van had disappeared. It was only seconds ago, but in the labyrinth of stacked containers the van had vanished.

"You didn't tell me we needed backup," Grace said as she stopped.

There was no point in pursuing. The van was probably off the island by now. "I had no idea she was going to run." I explained about Becky's phone.

"Do you have her number? We can pull her records and see who Misty was talking to."

I pulled my phone out of my pocket and a notification flashed on my screen. It was gone before I could read it and I scrolled through the contacts until Becky's name came up. I gave the number to Grace who wrote it down. While she tried to locate someone who could give her the last number that Becky's phone had called, I went back to my phone and read the notification. It was the reminder I had set for the meeting with the attorney.

"You look like you've seen a ghost," Grace said, turning to face me.

The phone was to her ear, and I guessed she was on hold. "I have a meeting with a lawyer in half an hour."

"That doesn't sound good."

"Custody thing."

"I don't guess you're going to get there by boat. Can I drive you?"

I hadn't expected the offer. "You sure? It's just downtown." I read her the address from my phone.

"No worries. I'll keep working this end. At our salaries, meetings with lawyers don't take very long. After that we'll figure out what to do about your missing girls."

I realized how bad that sounded. Not only had I lost the girl on the backside of Adams Key, now I had lost the girl I had saved, who apparently didn't want to be saved. The web was becoming more tangled by the minute. There was still no sign of the van as Grace pulled onto the MacArthur Causeway. Minutes later, we were downtown. We found the building and she pulled into a no-parking zone across the street.

"Go ahead. I got this."

We still hadn't heard back from the cell phone provider and until we did, there was nothing else we could do with Becky's phone on the bottom of the bay. Phone companies were notoriously unresponsive to requests for records without a warrant.

After losing the phone, I would have to try and get Martinez to reimburse her for the cost of it—another battle I would have to fight. I climbed out of the police cruiser and walked across the sidewalk, feeling out of place, dressed in my dark green park service shorts, khaki shirt, and boat shoes. It felt even stranger entering the lobby of the office building. Passing a marble fountain and several large paintings, I checked the directory and headed for the elevator wondering if I really deserved to see my own kid after losing two others in less than twenty-four hours.

Thankfully, I had the elevator to myself and when it stopped on the twentieth floor, I had an urge to head back down and run. Fighting through my anxiety, I crossed the plush carpet and entered the tall double doors of the attorney's office. A few minutes later, and ahead of several other better-dressed people in the waiting area, I was ushered into the office of Daniel J. Viscount, Esquire.

He barely acknowledged me as he leaned back in his desk chair and thumbed through a file which I hoped was mine since I figured we were on the clock the minute I walked in the door. Motioning me to a chair, he continued to read. I sat, fidgeting to get comfortable. Sitting in any attorney's office was intimidating, but this was clearly over my pay grade. I had tried the less ostentatious firms, but as soon as I mentioned the cartel that had firebombed my house, they kicked me up the ladder. I guessed I had reached the top.

Finally, the attorney set the file on the bare mahogany desk and looked at me.

"Cartels are bad for custody."

I couldn't believe I was going to be denied again. If he wouldn't take the case, I didn't know where else to turn. Fortunately, money, at least in the short term wasn't a problem. I was living rent free and had a company boat and truck. The feds covered my insurance and funded my pension plan. They even clothed me. The only expenses I had were food, which I had become pretty good at catching myself, and the occasional date with Justine. I sat there in silence waiting for him to continue.

"But, it looks like you've done the right things in the last year."

That was the first time a "but" had gone in my favor. "Okay," I stammered, wanting not to hope.

"I'm not saying this is going to be easy, and you'll probably have to settle for supervised visits for a while."

"That's okay." I had been expecting a no. Anything was better than that.

"So, if this is suitable, I have set an emergency hearing for tomorrow." He leaned over, wrote something on the back of his business card and handed it to me.

My heart started to race when he said tomorrow and I was about to pocket it, thinking it might be a phone number when he cleared his throat. When I turned the card over I saw a number with four zeros after it. I looked at him, but he had already picked up another file. Still staggered by the amount, I thanked him and was about to turn and leave the office when I saw the view from his floor-to-ceiling windows. He didn't seem to notice when I walked toward it. My five-figure fee probably covered a few minutes of admiring his office.

Facing east, his office had an unobstructed view of the upper bay and Miami Beach. Peeking from between the high-rise condos lining the water, I could see the Atlantic Ocean. That wasn't the view that had caught my attention; it was the cruise ships lining the north side of Dodge island and the grid of containers beyond. Daniel J. Viscount had probably never noticed the industrial section of his view or he surely would have raised his fee and moved to a better office. I found the park service green fabric covering my T-top and then looked back to where the van had gone. I panned my gaze over to South Beach and looked at the grid of streets.

I hadn't gotten a license plate, but I did notice the van had been customized. The signage and increased headroom made it stand out from the thousands of other white vans cruising Miami.

"Mr. Hunter?"

I took out my camera and shot a picture. "Nice view."

"Yes, it is."

I barely heard him as I ran out of the office, past the receptionist who was probably about to toss my file for not leaving a retainer, and to the elevator. I paced the luxurious carpet while I watched the lights above the door tick up. Finally, the car arrived. I got in and started down. The five stops on the way to the lobby were excruciating.

Most observers that knew who I had just met with probably thought I was running out of the building because of the fee, but it was the white van that I had seen that had me running.

8

I RAN ACROSS THE STREET TO THE MIAMI-DADE CRUISER. "THAT'S THE van that grabbed Misty," I said as I jumped into the passenger seat and thrust the phone in front of Grace.

She fumbled with the screen and I wanted to grab the phone from her but finally, after a few long seconds, she had zoomed into the block where the van was parked. "There're thousands of white vans in this city."

"The lettering looks the same. It had one of those wraps around the back and a high top, like they use for airport shuttles."

"Well, that narrows it down to a few hundred. I guess there's no harm. Let's go have a look."

"What about a helicopter?"

"Slow down, Kurt. We don't have any crime here, besides an unreliable girl's report of a *friend* who is missing."

She was right. After all, Misty had called the van to pick her up. I tried to lower my expectations and started squirming in my seat as she calmly checked the mirrors and pulled into traffic. "Shouldn't we call some backup?" My gut told me there was more to this.

"To check out a van that looks like every other shuttle in Miami? We need a little more than that."

She must have sensed my urgency and sped up, but it was still slow going. It was the middle of the afternoon now and traffic was heavy. I cringed when I saw the brake lights ahead on the MacArthur Causeway. Even if I could have talked her into turning on the lights and siren, there was nowhere to go. The shoulder was too narrow for the cars to pull over or for us to pass. If South Beach were a true island, with one way in and out, I would have felt better, but it was just the tip of Miami Beach. There were at least a half-dozen bridges the van could take to the mainland before they reached the Broward County line. A1A, the main artery running along the beach was my only saving grace. It was usually so congested that people took the closest bridge back to the mainland.

While we waited, I thumbed Daniel J. Viscount's business card, wondering how depleted my finances were going to be if and when this was over. I had three years before Allie was eighteen and could make her own decisions. With an hourly fee north of four hundred dollars, it was going to be a long few years. The attorney that referred me to him said that Viscount's background as a US attorney justified his paycheck. With the connections he had accrued over his years of service, he would hopefully be able to work some magic for me.

Finally, traffic started to move, but it was short-lived and stopped again when we hit Alton Avenue. Grace worked her way into the left-turn lane where we were stuck again, waiting for the light to change. I followed along on the map app on my phone as we turned left on Alton. A past case based out of the Miami Beach Marina was the extent of my South Beach experience. I looked back through my window and saw the tips of the masts from the sailboats docked at the marina through the narrow breaks in the high-rise condos and apartment buildings.

We were moving north now, close to the southern tip of the long stretch of real estate known as Miami Beach. Grace avoided the beachfront route and stayed on Alton, hugging the Intracoastal Waterway heading north.

The neighborhood was eclectic. Strip malls were interspersed with scaled-down versions of the larger chains stores. Many of the smaller stores had Kosher signs in the windows. Delis and liquor stores were prevalent. The area as a whole looked like a tropical New York—which in fact it was. We passed several newer art-deco style buildings and pulled over in a no-parking space adjacent to and across the street from where the van had been parked.

"It's gone," I said.

"You were hoping for...?"

I looked up and down the block. If the van had stopped here, there must have been a reason. "Must be that place," I said, getting out of the car. After scanning the other storefronts on the street, there was little doubt that on this street if there was foul play, it would happen at a "gentleman's club".

"Not so fast. You gonna run in there with your guns blazing... and what?" Grace asked.

I knew she was right in one regard and wrong in another. "I'll go in alone." She paused and nodded in agreement. The locals were already less than fond of the often overbearing Miami-Dade police, though in defense of local law enforcement—this was one hard area to work. Comprised of neighborhoods that resembled mini-countries, Dade County held factions of every ethnic group in the Caribbean blended with a newer mix of Eastern Europeans—most didn't get along.

Crossing the sidewalk, I stood in front of the door, noticing the placard with the club's hours. It appeared they were just about to open. I pushed the handle and found it unlocked, and was immediately assaulted by the sound of a driving bass and flashing lights. An electronic buzzer sounded, startling me when I entered. The door closed behind me and I stood in the entrance to the club. There was an empty chair on the left where a bouncer normally sat. A quick glance showed a vacant counter to the right with a selection of T-shirts and paraphernalia. Again, there was no one there and I suspected they were minimally staffed this early.

The layout was typical strip club. A curved stage with several brass poles jutted out over the carpeted floor. Chairs were pushed up against it with tables behind.

Glancing around, I saw no sign of life. I expected at least a couple of dancers and a bartender, but the club seemed empty. Moving to the back, I saw a closed door with "VIP Room" stenciled on the frosted glass. Crossing the room, I went to the door, finding it slightly ajar. Before I pushed it open, I saw small spots of a thick liquid covering the glass, some still wet and dripping. With just the tip of my finger, I slowly eased it open.

Blood splatter covered the room and a body lay prone on the floor. It was a young man and from the blood pooled around his head, there was no reason to rush for an ambulance. Feeling the bile rise in my stomach, I left the club and walked over to the driver's side of the cruiser. I took a deep breath as the window lowered. I'd been around several dead bodies in my recent past. The first few had been in the water long enough for it to scour them clean of any blood and they were clinical. The last had been gorier, but finding it in the water had helped. This was my first fresh kill.

"Dead guy."

Her door flew open, almost pushing me out of the way, and Grace ran to the entrance, pulling out her service weapon before entering. Her training overrode the fact that I had already checked the premises and, with her gun scanning the empty club, I walked in behind her. Satisfied we were alone, she assigned me to the front door and went to check the back—something I had failed to do. A minute later, she emerged, speaking into her phone as she approached.

"Medical examiner and forensics are on the way. You found the body, so I'm going to need a statement."

She was all business now, which was a good thing, because it was after five and Justine would be the tech. The two held a professional respect for each other, but there was something slightly off with their relationship. Justine gave me a hard time about the women I encountered in my cases, but it was just that. Though I had no idea what it was, there was something more between her and Grace. I didn't think it had anything to do with me.

"Now or later?" I asked.

"Why not while we wait. Walk me through what you did after you left the car."

It only took a few minutes. Grace followed behind me taking pictures with her phone and writing down what I said. We ended the tour at the VIP room and both looked at the dead man.

"Quite the party."

Dollar bills and empty glasses littered the floor and the handful of couches in the room. There were several champagne bottles on the side tables with condensation pooled underneath them. Music, if you could call it that, blared through hidden speakers and a disco ball still spun in the middle of the ceiling.

"Can't tell if there was a fight or just a party."

"I'm going with party. The furniture is all still standing," Grace said.

I concurred and leaned over to look at the body. He was probably in his mid-thirties, heavily tattooed with the pale complexion of someone who rarely saw the light of day. I suspected he worked here.

While we waited, I thought about Misty's stated career as a hostess and how with the van appearing here at a strip club, aside from her missing friend, she was now linked to a murder in South Beach. My analysis was interrupted by sirens—more than one vehicle from the sound of it. Seconds later, four officers entered the club. A little overkill for a single dead body, but no one had asked me.

In the room full of assault weapons and bulletproof vests, I was feeling out of place in my NPS uniform. Grace issued some orders and the club was quickly ringed with yellow crime scene tape. I wondered if it wasn't a good time to duck out and leave this to Miami-Dade when Justine walked in carrying her forensics case. Right behind her was Sid, the Jersey-bred, almost retired, nighttime medical examiner.

"You again? Can't imagine what you were fishing for in here."

His nasal accent was directed at me. It seemed every time he had seen me, there was a dead body between us. Usually I had found them out fishing the backwaters of the park. I caught Justine's eye and motioned my head toward the bar.

"Hey," I started.

"Funny meeting you and Wonder Woman here," she said.

"My runaway ran away again and we tracked her here."

"Funny, no bloodhounds outside, but there's Grace."

"You told me I needed to file a statement."

"So this is my fault?"

This was going nowhere with her on the defensive and I turned away.

"I get it. Just get fired up sometimes. How'd the lawyer thing go?" she asked.

Before I could reply, Sid called her over. She smiled. I wasn't sure if it was for my benefit or if it was because of the victim. My girl liked dead bodies.

While Sid examined the corpse, Justine started working the scene. The flash of her camera went off every few seconds as she placed numbered cards and recorded whatever evidence she saw. While she was occupied, I stepped outside to think. As if on cue, my phone vibrated. I didn't even have to look at the screen to know who it was.

"South Beach? Need a little sun and sand?"

Of course he knew where I was. "I had requested some personal time to see a lawyer about my daughter," I reminded him. There were a few seconds of silence while I waited for an apology. Before he could answer, I heard the thump, thump, thump of a helicopter close by. The Miami-Dade chopper came in low and hovered over the crime scene for a few seconds before moving away, in what I guessed was a search pattern looking for the van.

"And there are helicopters in your attorney's office?" Martinez spat.

With his resources, it wouldn't take much to find the chatter about the murder. "I kind of found a murder scene," I said. "At a strip club," I said, figuring I might as well get it all out now.

"Holy crap, Hunter," he said. "Get your ass out of there and let Miami-Dade handle it."

For once I agreed with him. Normally, I would fight him tooth and nail to remain active in an investigation. There was only one page of the rulebook that I knew. Section 9 Article 2 of the park service manual gave me authority to pursue cases outside of official park boundaries. I had used it more than once, but now the trail back to the park was thin. I promised to leave it to Miami-Dade and that I would be back on patrol in the morning and disconnected.

The officer working the entrance to the club gave me the once over when I approached the door and it took Grace to get me admitted back into the scene. I took this for a good sign that I would be dismissed. My only regret was leaving things like this with Justine, but as I looked over at the body, she was totally engrossed in helping Sid.

"I gotta go," I said to Grace and started for the door, figuring it would be better to call Justine later.

"Just don't leave town," Grace's attempt at comedy fell flat.

Fortunately for her, but not so much for me, I heard my name called. We both turned toward the duo working around the dead man. "Hunter, you'd better see this."

9

Suddenly the music and light show stopped and I looked around to see who was calling me. Grace's partner had arrived. I thought I had dodged that bullet, but he must have caught a ride with another unit.

"Got the bartender. Thought you cleared the building, Ranger Rick," her partner said.

I cringed when I heard him, but let the nickname go. After all, I had taken to calling him Dick Tracy. "I took a quick look around, saw the body, and got Grace."

"Not the way we do it. He was out back in the beer cooler." He said, walking him over to a table, he started questioning him.

It turned out he was the only employee here this early. There were two girls assigned to work the small private party before opening, who had disappeared. It was just champagne, so he had set up the room and left them to prepare for the regular opening.

"You got any info on who booked the party? How many, where they were from, who paid— that kind of thing?" Tracy asked.

"There should be something in the office."

We walked together towards a partially concealed door next to a hallway which looked like it led to the dressing rooms. The office was too small for all of us, so we waited outside while the bartender retrieved the information. He came back a minute later with a clipboard. "Name's Alex. Paid up front. *Seductress Charters* is the name on the credit card."

"Contact information?" Grace asked.

He wrote something down on a piece of paper and handed it to her. "What was the name of the boat the girl said they were aboard?" Grace asked.

"Yeah, she said they lived aboard *Spindrift,* but the party was aboard *Temptress.*" I leaned over the small rectangular piece of paper.
"

It had an address at the Miami Beach Marina, a place I was unfortunately too familiar with. I walked over to the VIP room to see how Sid and Justine were doing. What had once appeared to be a strictly Miami-Dade affair had circled back to me.

"Give us a few more minutes," Sid said, shooing me out of his way. "Almost done here."

He moved around the body, doing whatever Medical Examiners do. Right now he was searching the dead man's pockets. He fished a wallet out of the front and handed it to Justine. She laid it on the counter next to the receipt and carefully extracted a driver's license.

"Jensen Stillhouse," she said.

The name didn't make the man on the floor any less dead.

"He's the manager," the bartender said. He stood in the doorway.

"We can deal with the rest at the morgue. Let's get him out of here," Sid called over to two deputies standing by the door. He must have seen the question on our faces. "He was strangled."

"Why all the blood then?"

His look told me I would have to wait for that answer.

It took four of us to get the dead man into the body bag and load him onto the gurney. Finally, the deputies wheeled him out and Sid started packing up his equipment. I thought about the last few bodies I had found, glad that this one was not in the park and I wouldn't have to sit in on the autopsy.

Once the body was removed, Justine started her real work. She had already chalked the outline of the dead man on the floor. Now she started to move around, taking pictures, and picking up anything that could remotely be considered evidence. With the mess lying around, there was a lot of it. I had to admire her as she worked; besides her efficiency, she moved with a cat-like grace, her body toned by hours of paddleboarding.

"There's another one of those VIP rooms back there," Dick Tracy said. "Really? You want to cuddle at a crime scene, it's probably open."

I ignored him and whispered a quick joke that only Justine could hear at his expense. Whatever tension had been between us earlier was gone. Maybe because Grace had disappeared into the back, but more likely because few things got my girl excited like a dead body.

"What about security footage?"

Grace gave me a stone-cold stare. I had received the same from Justine on other occasions when I overstepped my bounds and wondered if they taught it at the Miami-Dade police academy. I stepped back to acknowledge her authority. I had to remember that we were in Miami Beach and not Biscayne National Park, where our roles would have been reversed. This wasn't our first rodeo and I knew better.

"You can't be putting security cameras in a club like this. Clientele sees them, they won't be back," the bartender said.

"You saw the group. Who were they?"

"Young players would be my guess. This guy Alex books them in here pretty regularly. I think he's a big shot with the boosters at the U."

"Sounds like they were underage," I said. He dropped his head to the floor.

"We're not ABC," Grace said, glaring at me again.

"Y'all need to move on," Justine said. I need to start collecting fingerprints." She pulled double gloves on before starting. "Can't be too careful in here."

We left her to her work, and went to the bar to plan out next step.

We knew where the boat was now, but that became secondary when Grace's radio went off. The helicopter had found the van.

10

With her headphones on, Justine was in her own world, processing the crime scene. I took one more longing look and left with Grace. "I'll follow you," I said, before realizing that I had no transportation.

"Maybe better if you rode along. This is my jurisdiction and I don't want you going rogue on me," she said.

For a second, I was about to look behind me and see if Susan McLeash had somehow slipped in and that was who she was addressing. I had to accept that I had gone slightly beyond my authority before, and as long as I was still involved, it shouldn't hurt my ego if she was in charge. I went around the car and opened the passenger door. Martinez would certainly approve.

"Thanks, Ranger Rick," Grace's partner said, sliding by me and taking the shotgun seat.

I took a deep breath and tried not to react to him. To add insult to injury, I pulled the lever for the back door and found it locked. I had to tap on the passenger window to get Dick's attention before the electronic lock disengaged and I could open it. As Grace pulled away from the curb, I sat behind the steel screen thinking I was being treated like a criminal. Dick was listening to the radio, giving Grace directions from the helicopter pilot's report. I leaned forward trying to see the screen of the phone. The steel mesh blocked my view and finally, I sat back. Grace had the lights on, but no siren and with traffic pulling over, we easily navigated through the streets of South Beach.

"It's moving again," the pilot's voice came through the radio.

I couldn't help myself and peered through the grill. I knew where the van had stopped. "He just left the marina."

"Duh."

"We need to split up. I can take the marina and you guys follow the van," I said.

"Not on your life, Ranger boy. This is our territory."

"At least check the marina. We know the boat names. We can check with the dockmaster. Maybe he dropped some of the guys off."

"He's making sense," Grace said.

"Yeah well, I'm calling in backup."

Dick Tracy got on the radio and called for both boat and vehicle backup. I had to admit serious LEO envy, watching him summon the full power of Miami-Dade. I wasn't really sure if the park service was asset poor or if it was Martinez juggling the books to make himself look good, but I had to beg for everything and that more often than not involved Miami-Dade.

Although, the view through the front windshield was obscured, the side windows were clear and I was able to track our progress. Dick Tracy sat in the passenger seat, calling out the turns as we passed the on-ramp for the causeway. When he called out a right turn, I had a moment of deja vu as we entered the Miami Beach Marina. Home port of the *Big Bang*, the facility and adjacent bar had been the scene of a previous case. Before I could relive the moment when Susan McLeash had shot my primary suspect, the front doors opened and Grace and her partner started toward the dock. I had a moment of panic when I thought the doors were still locked, but the handle opened and I took off after them.

I knew my way around the marina and cast a glance at the bar, half expecting to see Gordy, the owner of *Bottoms Up Boat Cleaning*, as we ran toward the docks. Fortunately, the happy-hour crowd was two-deep at the bar and I passed without incident. I followed the Miami-Dade detectives down the seawall and stopped at a small building.

"I know the dockmaster," I said, moving to the door.

"Whatever, Ranger Rick," Dick Tracey said, removing his badge from his pocket and pushing past me. Justine had given me the nickname out of affection and I cringed again when he used it. We reached the small office and I decided to wait outside and let the detective pull his macho cop act by himself. A minute later, he flashed me a grin as we followed the dockmaster toward the locked gate.

"The *Temptress* docks down there," the teenage boy said, punching a code into the controller to the side of the gate marked Pier 4 in bold letters. "Slip forty-seven."

We left him standing there and took off down the dock. As we moved toward the end, the boats became bigger and more expensive. I could only wonder what the party boat looked like. We reached the slip number and stood staring at water. The *Temptress* was gone.

Glancing down at the dock, I saw something red and wet. "Over here," I called to Grace. Seconds later, the three of us were hovering over a trail of blood.

"Whoever this was, they were moving in the direction of the boat," Dick Tracy said.

I looked at the blood and, recalling my training from binge watching *CSI*, recognized the teardrop shaped droplets and knew he was right. Again, I tried my plea, "We need to split up." It wasn't Grace so much as her partner, but I knew I'd be better off on my own. They were homicide detectives; that's what they did—solve murders. I was more interested in saving the two live girls. The blood was surely evidence, if not a clue, and I texted Justine to come down when she was finished at the club. realizing as soon as I hit *send* that I should have had Grace request her presence.

I walked away from the scene just as a Miami-Dade police boat pulled into the marina. Grace flagged them down and a few minutes later, the two detectives were aboard and the boat took off. I wasn't sure if they were chasing the van or the *Temptress*; they could be chasing unicorns for all I knew. Glad to be rid of them, I waited until they had rounded the southern point and were out of sight before walking casually down the dock, not realizing when I had passed through the gate, that it had a self-closer. I heard it lock behind me. Before I could think of a story to tell the dockmaster, a woman approached, pushing a wheelbarrow full of provisions.

I stepped back as she punched a code into the keypad. When she struggled to get the wheelbarrow through the gate, I seized the opportunity. Reaching in front of her, I grabbed the gate, and held it open. She smiled and continued down the dock. I took a quick look around and followed. She stopped next to the vacant slip the *Temptress* had occupied. "Can I ask you a few questions?"

"Sure," she said, boarding a sleek sailboat. "If you help me load."

I jumped at the opportunity, assuring myself it was not because of her translucent blue eyes shaded by a white visor, which showed off her blond hair, or her slender body, barely concealed in a tight-fitting tennis outfit. It was because this kind of interaction was much more productive than an interview. She introduced herself as Donna and I grabbed the top box and handed it down to her. It was a slow process, as I could only ask a question every time she came back out for another box. By the time we had finished unloading the provisions, I had a few answers.

The boat she was provisioning was an eighty-foot luxury sailboat. When I asked about the *Temptress*, she turned away. I was about to follow up on the questions when I saw Justine coming down the dock. I handed Donna a card and went to the gate to let her in. Together we walked back to the empty slip.

"What'd you do with Miami-Dade's finest?" she asked, looking around the empty dock.

"They're off chasing the van or the boat. I'm not sure."

She laughed. "I heard something on the scanner that it was reported heading toward Key Biscayne. What about their cruiser? It's still in the parking lot."

"They hopped a ride on a police boat." I said.

"Probably makes sense. Be faster than driving."

The Rickenbacker Causeway connected Key Biscayne with the mainland but, in order to reach it, they would have had to backtrack through downtown, making a large U-turn. While I was figuring drive times, Justine had spotted the blood and placed her case down next to it. She removed some yellow numbers and snapped a few pictures before touching any evidence. "You guys didn't track through here, did you?"

Before I could answer her, I saw trouble coming.

"What happened? You didn't tell me you were a cop," the woman from the sailboat said, walking right through the path of blood.

Justine's claws came out. She looked up at the woman, but turned to me with a roll of crime scene tape in her hand. I knew what to do, and ushered Donna away from Justine. "Please, ma'am, this is an active crime scene."

"What's this 'ma'am stuff'? I told you my name was Donna."

Justine looked up from the blood and glared at both of us.

"Okay, Donna. Let's move over here and let her work." We moved toward the power pedestal.

"Crime scene..." Justine scolded. "There're likely prints there from when they disconnected from the shore services.

I scolded myself for not thinking about that and started walking Donna back to her boat. "Do you know the people that own the *Temptress*?" I asked, figuring if I was already in trouble, I might as well get some info out of it.

"Reese Rosen," she said bitterly. "*Seductress Charters*. He owns everything docked on this pier."

It added up. "Charters?"

"Luxury at its finest. All the bells and whistles. My husband and I run them."

"So you know where the *Temptress* is?"

"Alex is in charge of that group."

"Do you have an itinerary and manifest?"

"You could probably ask my husband. I just stock 'em and make sure the entertainment's right."

Before I could comment on the "entertainment", I followed her glance to the gate where a man was struggling to get a hand truck through the narrow opening. He was the size of an offensive lineman and when I held the gate for him, I saw what looked like a championship ring. Seeing him as able to fill the A-gap and screen me from his flirtatious wife and Justine, I followed him to the boat.

"About time you showed. The ranger here has been helping me," Donna said.

"Howdy howdy," he said, easily lifting two cases of beer from the wheelbarrow and crossing nimbly to the boat. "What's up next door?" he asked, glancing at Justine. "Hey, girl," he called over.

I followed his gaze and had a minute of jealousy when I saw him smile. Justine was bent over by the pedestal, dusting for prints. If it wasn't an awkward situation, I would have smiled, too. "Can you tell me anything about the *Temptress*?"

There was a flicker of something in his eyes. "If she got out on time, she'd be clearing International waters about now," he said, turning back to the boat. "Right, Donna?"

She turned, grabbed a case of the beer Alex had just brought aboard, and disappeared down the companionway. Alex continued to unload the half dozen cases. There was some urgency in the way they were working and I expected they would be pulling out soon.

"Got a charter?"

"Always, dude. Some sail, some motor, whatever works."

"Is the *Temptress* one of yours?"

"Everything this side of the dock belongs to Mr. Rosen." He turned back to Donna with the last box and disappeared into the cabin.

It didn't seem like I was going to get anything else out of him so I walked back to Justine and watched her work. Asking was probably not going to get me any answers and I thought about the timing.

"How much longer?"

Justine looked up at me. "You can't rush these things."

I wasn't going to push her if she was working. "I'm going to check with the dockmaster about something."

"Cool," she said without looking up.

I knew she liked to work alone—one of the reasons she worked the night shift. With Justine occupied, and Alex and Donna out of sight, I was happy to walk away. I reached the gate and ran into a girl pushing a cart of dive gear. She wore a full wetsuit, with the top part peeled off revealing a bikini top. My first thought was Abbey, a woman who's body I had found back in the bay. She had been killed several piers away for uncovering an insurance scam to blow the *Big Bang*. But this woman had blond hair and was very much alive. We smiled at each other and I continued to the dockmaster's building, but instead of going in, I walked past it, heading to the bar. The diver had given me an idea.

11

He wasn't hard to find, not even for an experienced special agent. Gordy rarely left the marina. It was his place of business, and had a bar—all that he required. His radar must have been running on high with the police activity because as soon as he saw me, he ducked behind several women he was talking to. It wasn't a bold move, just a natural reaction for a sleazebag who used the premise of a legitimate business to exploit women.

Abbey had worked for Gordy and was murdered on the job. Thanks to Susan killing the main suspect, his involvement was never really clear. The case was closed, but not solved.

Gordon was his real name and boats were his game, or so he said. *Bottom's up Boat Cleaning* used attractive women to clean hulls and detail boats here in the marina. Cleaning the boats in the water, at their slip, was far less expensive than dry-dock, and there were obvious perks to the right kind of owner or captain having a hot bikini-clad woman around, cleaning the decks and stainless.

"Hello, Gordon," I said as I approached the bar. He was still playing possum, but knew I had seen him. "Nothing to do with you, just have a few general marina-type questions," I said, trying to put him at ease. It would have been a stretch if he was involved in this, but he knew what went on here.

"Special Agent," he said, rising to his full height.

He was several inches taller than my six feet, but had gone to pot. "Buy you a drink?"

"Nah, but we can talk over there."

He put his three-quarters full highball to his lips and took a long sip. When he put it down, it had less than a quarter left. "You sure about that drink?"

"What the hell." He motioned to the bartender.

I removed my wallet, ordered a club soda for myself, and paid, telling the bartender to keep the change from the twenty I handed him. There was no way Martinez was going to reimburse me for this, so I might as well toss away a fe more dollars and make a friend. With our drinks in hand, Gordy led us to an out-of-the-way table behind a large potted palm. I knew it blocked the view from the bar, having used the same plant to hide before.

"Let's skip the pleasantries. What can I do for you?" Gordy said, slurping half the drink in one gulp, letting me know he could end this meeting with one more sip.

"Pier 4? Rosen's charter boats."

"What about them?"

"That's what I'm asking you."

"It's all for the U," he said.

I remembered the bartender at the club saying something about the group being from the U. Florida residents wore their college loyalties on their sleeves: Seminoles, Gators, Hurricanes. I kind of got it, but Northern California is not ripe with football rivalries. These folks were fanatics. If you went to one of the big three, everyone knew it. Jobs, promotions, and all kinds of favors were granted from alumni to alumni. It would be a rare occurrence to find a Gator hiring a Seminole if there was another Gator in the room.

"Do you work for him?"

"He uses a more traditional service. There're enough women floating around that dock, he doesn't need to pay a premium for his cleaning needs. Besides," he said, making a chopping motion with his right hand, "I'm a 'nole."

With this information, I tried to dig deeper, knowing he would throw Rosen and Alex under the bus for no other reason than they were Hurricanes. Every Florida State alum still sought revenge for Wide Right. "Whatever you can tell me. There're two missing girls I'm trying to track down."

He opened up, even to the point of ignoring his drink. "Rosen is a big-time booster. He's all in for the U. Alex and that bimbo wife of his are sucking the straw from both ends, trying to sway high school recruits and then keep them happy for a few years hoping the dumber ones'll sign him as their agent if they make it to the pros."

I had heard on the radio something about National Signing Day coming up. "Guess next week's big for them."

"You could say this is their busy season," he said, finishing his drink. "That help you out?"

I had a few more questions, but didn't feel like paying the toll and buying another drink. The information he had given me was a big start and, if I needed more, I knew where to find him.

"Appreciate your help," I said, rising and extending my hand. He blew off the handshake in favor of making a sucking sound with his straw.

I continued with my original plan and started walking to the dockmaster's office. It would help with the timeline if the marina had any information about the boats that had gone out yesterday, especially the one that Misty and her friend had hastily disembarked from.

I entered the air-conditioned office and waited for the boy to get off the phone. He held up a finger, letting me know he would only be a minute. I studied him as he talked. He was carefully, and expensively groomed. His haircut and product alone were probably half my paycheck. The earrings he wore in both ears looked more real than fake and I couldn't help but notice the chain around his neck. If it was real, it had cost a fortune. He looked younger than his size and had the stubble of a carefully outlined beard.

Dockmaster was one of those kinds of jobs where you could line your pockets if you were cool and could keep your mouth shut. It was like being a doorman in New York City—tip heavy. Generally, they were punks. Through my years on patrol, I had run into enough two-bit drug dealers and make-believe businessmen to learn some of their quirks. One that I used now was silence. Fearing their empire was about to crumble, they talked. Especially with the younger variety, they couldn't stand quiet, and if you left a vacuum, they would fill it.

He set the phone down and introduced himself.

"Kyler Smith."

I began by asking about the boats down on Pier 4 and he started fidgeting. I stayed quiet, counting to myself and making a private bet that by the time I reached ten, he would be talking. He cracked at eight—not bad for his age.

"They don't need to check in and out."

"But they ask for favors and you know what's going on here." I saw something in his expression. "I'm not after you or any of your buddies. Just trying to figure out a timeline for a crime."

"No worries, but I wasn't working here yesterday."

I thanked him and was about to leave when the light reflected off the gold chain around his neck.

"That for the U?"

He fingered the heavy medallion hanging on a thick gold chain. Half orange and half green, the school colors, the over-sized U-shaped logo glittered in the light.

"Turnover Chain, man."

I had seen the chain during some of the Hurricane games. It was awarded to a defensive player after they intercepted a pass or recovered a fumble. The bling was intended to bring some of the swagger back to a program that was once famous for it and was now in the midst of a twenty-year drought. It had worked until the team caved in the last three games of the season, dropping from a National Championship contender to a double-digit ranking. I stared at its weight and shape while we talked, and calculated its effect as a weapon.

"Alex is big with them, isn't he?" I asked.

"He wrote me a letter of recommendation and gave me this when I got accepted. Heading there in the fall."

"You gonna play ball?" I asked. He was a big kid.

"Nah, can't hang with those dudes. I'm going to major in business."

It looked like he had a pretty good start on that path. "So, he's got some juice over there?"

"Dude's tight. Used to play back in the day. I think they even gave him one of the real chains after the season."

I thanked him and gave him one of the obligatory cards with instructions to call if he remembered anything. The conversation had been productive, but I got the feeling toward the end, especially when Alex's name came up, that he was getting protective.

Justine was just about wrapped up when I reached the empty slip. Hoping she had cooled off a little, I started to help take down the tape and collect the numbered placards. It was time to make peace and the best way to do that was with a body.

"I have an idea for the murder weapon."

She gave me a "this isn't going to work" look and continued picking up her supplies, but I knew she was curious. "You went to the U, right?"

"Yeah, but what's that got to do with this? I got a real degree in Forensic Sciences, not like those guys."

My girl was a geek, and I loved her for it. "I hear you." I'd been around Justine and a football game before, when we spent New Year's together. The two didn't mix. I stashed my idea for now and went with a sure thing. "Think we can test the blood against the pieces of clothes I got from Misty and the other girl?"

"That and fingerprints would be my next step."

There was something going on here that was over my pay grade. We'd had a few fights, and they were usually work related. She usually said her piece and was done. This was unusual. I had one bullet left. "Can we go to the morgue when you're done?"

"I'll require dinner first."

"You got it," I smiled to myself.

Carrying one of Justine's cases, we walked back to the gate. From this side, it had a paddle handle and no lock which allowed me to push it open with my elbow and hold the gate for her. I took a quick look back to see if Alex or Donna had surfaced, but there was no sign of them.

We walked to the crime scene van. "I came over on the boat with Misty. Can I get a ride?"

She nodded and placed both cases in the back. Justine was quiet as we pulled out of the parking lot and onto Alton Road. She was about to turn when I saw a souvenir store. "Can we stop?"

"Really?"

She indulged me and parked, but pulled out her phone instead of getting out. "I could use your help." She was about the same size as the club manager.

She got out and, tossing me a look with a little attitude, we entered the store. My skin instantly started to crawl. The walls were covered with vulgar T-shirts and hats. Towels, shot glasses, and bric-a-brac covered the tables and counters. No wonder she wanted to stay in the van.

"You looking for something specific?" Justine asked.

A trace of a smile crossed her face and I knew she was curious. "Here," I said, leading her to a display of gaudy gold chains. I picked up several and measured the opening in the U against my recollection of the dead man's neck. I held one up to Justine's to get a better idea.

"Just because I went to the U, doesn't mean I'm wearing one of those. Embarrassing, if you ask me. We were better off swaggerless."

Ignoring her, I tried another, this time placing it against her skin. "Got it."

"Oh my God! Killed by a Turnover Chain, how fitting."

12

WE LEFT THE SOUVENIR STORE WITH THE LARGEST TURNOVER CHAIN they sold. My personal expenses were starting to add up after buying Gordy a drink and now the chain. Martinez would never reimburse me for it and Justine wanted nothing to do with it. I guessed the only thing it would be good for after we were done at the ME's office was a fishing weight. Dangling the heavy logo around my hand, I played with its weight; it could do some damage.

"Can you see if Sid's around?" I asked as we reached the van, expecting a more welcoming response to my request if she asked him.

"You still owe me dinner." She fingered the heavy medallion. "This bling ain't gonna cut it."

She picked up her phone, located his number, and pressed connect. The call went to his voicemail and I sat back in the passenger seat wondering what I could suggest for dinner that I could keep down if I was able to see Sid. I really didn't want to sit in on the autopsy, but the only way to know if my theory was correct was to try it. Justine was a fan of breakfast for dinner, and I thought that might be my best bet. "How about breakfast?"

"Think you're gonna get lucky?"

"No, for dinner. But, yeah I'd like that, too."

Our relationship had gotten comfortable over the past few months. There was a mutual trust we shared and the only fly in the ointment was the women that I couldn't shake. Grace Herrera was more than attractive, but at least she was all business. Some of the women involved in my last few cases were also knockouts and a whole lot less appropriate. I knew she trusted me; it was the other women she had a problem with.

She nodded, made a left onto A1A, and headed north for a few blocks. Turning onto a side street, she parked in front of an omelet place with a breakfast-served-all-day sign in the window. "How's this?"

"Cool." I said, already thinking about what would stay down. The closest I'd been to a dead body out west was the road kill we were tasked with removing from the park roads. Since being assigned to Biscayne National Park, I had found three bodies, four if you count the man at the club. Fortunately, their condition had been a gradual introduction to human death and decay. The visceral seawater of the bay had washed any sense of life from the first two. They had been in the water long enough for the crabs and fish to get to them. The last, had been mangled by a crocodile, but had still ended up in the water where, after even a few hours, the sea had removed any evidence of life.

Witnessing the first few autopsies was a clinical experience. I suspected having to watch Sid open up the man from the club would be different—there would be blood, at least what was left.

"I'll just have a plain omelet with toast," I said, catching the eye of the waitress. The menu had twenty combinations and enough a-la-carte ingredients for another hundred.

"Worried about the body?"

"Yeah. My first almost live one."

Justine ordered a combination of meat and veggies that I'm not sure I could have held down—even without the autopsy. We sat quietly waiting for our food. "You ready for the race this weekend?" I asked, trying to steer the conversation away from work. Living my job had been my downfall before. I had been given another chance and was hoping for a better result.

"Won't really know until it's over," she said.

The waitress brought our food and I took small bites of mine while watching Justine inhale hers. I figured from what she'd told me of her training that she had probably done six or eight miles this morning, many at a pretty high intensity. I was proud and a little envious of her; I could barely stand up on a board, let alone race ten miles in open water on one. For the time being at least, I was better off in a kayak.

Her phone rang just as we were finishing up. It was Sid, who gave us the go-ahead to come by. He didn't say whether he had started, finished, or where he was with the body. I steeled myself for the worst.

Fifteen minutes later, we pulled up to the medical examiners' building behind Jackson Memorial Hospital. I put on the medallion and got out of the van, but didn't get two feet before Justine smacked me and told me to stow it. The fact that the garish symbol represented her alma mater was embarrassing enough, but it was even worse hanging around her boyfriend's neck.

We entered the building and went downstairs to the autopsy rooms. We walked inside and stood next to a stainless-steel table. Everything about the room was harsh. From the lighting to the flooring, everything gleamed.

"Just in time for the cut," Sid said as he entered the room.

The body was still in the bag it had been transported in. He might have been excited, but I wasn't. With his nasal Jersey accent and stooped posture, he bent over the table and started dictating. Justine was shoulder to shoulder with him, assisting. I stood as far back as I thought I could get away with, waiting patiently as they removed the bag and rolled the body onto the table. Sid started dictating again, calling out details of the deceased. I guessed it was all standard procedure and I fingered the medallion in my pocket, waiting for him to complete the posterior examination. When they rolled the body onto his back, I stood stoically, hoping my dinner would remain where it was. The blood had dried and it wasn't as gruesome as I had imagined. Finally, Sid looked at me.

"The neck shows signs of strangulation," he said, pointing out the light bruising where the murder weapon had tightened around it. "But, he bled out." Sid took an instrument and folded a piece of skin back revealing the severed artery.

"I have an idea," I said.

"I don't suppose you're going to sit through this whole thing. Let's see what you have."

I pulled the chain out and approached the table, walking behind the man's head.

"Ah, the Turnover Chain," he said, shaking his head.

I was surprised he knew what it was.

"It was all good when they were winning, but drop a few games and the luster wears off. You look like an idiot when you're jumping around on the sidelines with that thing bouncing on your neck and your team is two touchdowns down to Virginia."

"Point taken." I held the U-shaped logo out, trying to size it before I fit it. All I could think of was Johnny Cochran's famous line: "If the glove doesn't fit, you must acquit."

"Parcells and Belichik wouldn't have any of it," Sid said. "The '86 Giants didn't need a chain, they just lined up the ambulances."

Sid, was full of surprises. I looked up at him and tried to steady my hands as I placed the huge U over the man's neck. "Fits."

"And the Turnover Chain is the murder weapon," Sid said. "I guess they never thought about that when they made it."

"Now we just need the real one. There've got to be thousands out there," Justine said.

I removed the pendant, took it to the sink across from the table, and washed the blood from it. "I've got an idea where to look."

"I thought you were tossing this one to Miami-Dade?" Justine asked.

"It's not so much him," I looked down at the corpse. "There're two living girls out there and I think this is all tied together."

I pulled out my phone and started for the door.

"Calling your buddy Grace?" Justine asked.

I shrugged. Sooner or later she was going to have to either get over this or tell me what the baggage between them was. Once outside the autopsy room, I glanced back through the glass, but her head was down. Turning away, I pressed connect and waited. The phone rang several times, then went to voicemail. I left a message to call me and stood in the small office wondering what to do now.

Justine would be tied up here for a few hours at least and Martinez would be all over me tomorrow morning for spending the day in Miami. Unless something happened fast, he'd have me back on patrol. I remembered the blood on the dock and the empty slip at the marina. Maybe a quick patrol wouldn't hurt.

I knocked on the door and entered the lab. Justine looked up and met my eye, as if she was daring me to tell her I was meeting Grace. Fortunately, I didn't have to see if this would be a defining moment in our relationship. "I'm going to run by the marina and see if the *Temptress* has come back." I almost added, alone, but decided that would just be throwing fuel on a fire that wasn't really burning. "You guys look like you have a few hours. I can come back at midnight."

She smiled, "Say hi to the boys from the U."

I took that as an okay and left before Grace called me back. The night air was a relief, not only from the autopsy, but from the friction with Justine. I looked around the lot and realized I'd been tagging along with Miami-Dade and had ridden here with Justine—I only had my boat. Pulling my phone out, I found the Uber app and dialed up a ride. Thankfully, there was a language barrier and the drive was quiet.

Traffic was light in the interlude between happy hour and the late-night exodus from the South Beach clubs. We reached Dodge Island a few minutes later and I directed the driver to where I had docked earlier. It had only been half a day, but felt like much longer. The lights of the marina were less than a quarter mile across the channel—there was no reason to change plans.

After crossing the Intracoastal, I tied off toward the end of the empty fuel dock and was halfway to Pier 4 when I decided to turn back and grab the binoculars. I felt out of place walking along the seawall in my uniform, but everyone else was so absorbed in what they were doing, they barely noticed me. Several dog walkers gave me a head nod, which I returned and continued toward Pier 4.

The marina was laid out with at least a dozen piers jutting into the Intracoastal Waterway at ninety-degree angles to where I stood. One at a time, I stopped, trying to get the best view of Rosen's yachts without being seen. The best vantage point turned out to be two piers away, where I sat on a bench and placed the binoculars to my eyes. Bright lights hit me as I focused on the dock. The marina and many of the boats were typically well lit, but there was a halo around Pier 4. The yachts came into view as I fine-tuned the focus. One by one, I checked out each boat, pausing at the empty slip where the *Temptress* birthed. They were all lit, reminding me of the lines of sportfishing boats on display closer to the entrance. And as I scanned the docks, I saw there was quite a party going on.

I had noticed the hip-hop beat before I sat down, but now, watching the bodies on the decks of the boats swaying to the rhythm, I knew where it came from. Scantily clad "hostesses" were dancing with boys that looked too big for their young faces. Alex came into view, passing out insulated tumblers. The recruiting party was in full swing.

I panned the binoculars back to the closest boat to the seawall trying to single out Misty, and I found her several boats over. Even from this distance, I could tell she had applied a ton of makeup to cover the bruises—but at least she was alive. If I knew what her friend looked like, I would have tried to find her as well, instead, I kept an eye out for a girl with matching bruises.

I watched as Alex called out to a group of the boys. They sauntered over to him and he opened a box. They converged on him like the swarming defense they would probably become, and one boy held something over his head. It caught the light and I saw the real Turnover Chain.

13

I found myself staring at what could have been the murder weapon, now being passed around by a group of boys emulating the sideline dance. If it were indeed the murder weapon, there would be no forensics—too many hands had touched it. I sat back, watching the party, trying to think of a way to isolate the murderer. The only thing I was certain of was that he was part of the party. There were several other girls besides Misty with bruises that showed through the skillfully applied makeup. Whether intentionally or not, they seemed to cluster together in an attempt to protect each other. I would have liked to talk to them, but even if I had the authority to walk over and start asking questions, it wasn't the right time. The best I could do was to document the party. We had a murder, a murder weapon, several suspects, but no motive. Dancing in front of me were a bunch of soon-to-be-famous prospects, any one of whom could have committed the crime.

I was too far away for my phone's camera to get clear pictures, even with the telephoto setting. Moving to the next pier, I tried to position myself, but the light and definition of the few pictures I tried were poor. There was a line between how valuable the pictures would be and the cost of getting caught in the process. I decided if the murderer was there, the line moved toward the risky side. I moved over to the adjacent pier and using the largest zoom possible, started taking pictures. They wouldn't win any awards, but after reviewing the first few, I could make out the faces.

I was about halfway through when someone approached the locked gate and let themselves in. It appeared to be a uniformed security guard. He went directly to Alex as if this weren't the first time they had danced together. After a few heated words, Alex disappeared below decks and the music was turned down several notches. It was still pretty loud, but the dock was no longer vibrating. With the party over, I hurried to photograph everyone. I figured I'd wait around a few minutes and see if there was anyone below that I had missed.

Just as I was about to move, I saw a large, well-lit boat pull into the channel. The music coming from it blended with the turned-down music on the dock, making the overall effect louder. The security guard ran back to the boat and started screaming something to the captain who was in the middle of backing the boat into the slip. He ignored him until it was safely tied off, then to the jeers of the crowd, cut the music. I panned the binoculars over the transom of the boat. The *Temptress* was back.

I pulled the phone from my pocket and took pictures of everyone on deck, then put the binoculars to my eyes looking for anything that I might have missed. Surprisingly for the park service's budget, they were a high-quality, light-enhancing model and I was able to see detail in the shadows invisible to the naked eye. I moved the glasses past several couples making out, cataloguing their location in my mind to photograph when they moved into the light. Last I moved them to the helm.

It looked like the dockmaster, now dressed in a white shirt with gold braids and epaulets, was running the boat. The young captain was alone at the helm, the party having already abandoned him. As I watched him shut down the motors, I could tell he was not enjoying himself.

He sat at the helm, looking around at the party. When his eyes found Misty, dancing with one of the recruits a few boats over, they stayed there. He clearly knew her and was so focused that he missed Alex board the boat. The former player climbed the ladder and stood next to him. I was surprised to see they were close to the same height. They were soon deeply engrossed in a heated conversation.

Sliding around to get a better view, I realized how suspicious I looked standing on a seawall at a marina in South Beach with the binoculars, and stuffed them into my cargo pocket. I had accomplished much of my goal without being identified and decided not to push my luck when I saw the boy rise.

The party, although toned down, continued. He left the boat and started down the dock. I watched him glance over at Misty again before pushing the gate open with quite a bit more force than was required. Jealousy had been motive for plenty of murders and that's what this looked like. I decided to follow him.

I had to resist the urge to run, knowing he was coming toward me, and walked toward a dark spot. Sliding into the shadows, I thought I had been unobserved, but the figure was walking right toward me. Still in the shadows, I was close enough to see him clearly now and confirmed he was the dockmaster. Apparently, the kid I had met before was moonlighting for Alex. Moving further into the shadows, I hugged the wall trying to remain hidden.

He walked into the recess and stopped. Trying to control my breath, I waited and watched him pull out his phone. Seconds later, I could hear the whining as he tried to convince whomever was on the other end of the line that he wasn't done for the night. Apparently his pleas fell on deaf ears and he went back through the gate and started walking toward the *Temptress*

I stayed put for a few minutes to see what he was up to. The dockmaster / captain was the same age as the kids partying on the dock. I could smell the resentment, and sympathize with him. As cocky as he was, for his age, he had done well. The kids on the boat were gifted and, some had probably put in a lot of work to get where they were, but I suspected the party was for a different kind of student athlete and I use that term loosely. The whole recruiting scam was a huge entitlement.

The music stopped and, turning back to the dock, I saw the *Temptress* loaded with the entire group pull out of the slip. Moving the party into the middle of the Intracoastal might put them out of reach of security, but not Miami-Dade, and I didn't want to be around when they showed up.

I had a lot of pictures to go through and decided that I was done here. Reaching my boat unobserved, I got in, released the lines and idled into the main channel. If anyone saw me now, I was a ways from the marina.

Accelerating enough to overcome the current, I started toward Government Cut. Once I reached the last marker, I dropped out of gear and pulled out my phone to call Justine. The boat spun in the current and I had to make a correction. Just as I was going to press connect, I heard a loud roar and watched the red and green lights of the *Temptress* coming toward me at full speed. I dropped the phone on the seat next to me and simultaneously cut the wheel and pushed down the throttle, barely escaping the path of the boat. I could only watch as the triple outboards dug in and accelerated toward open water. Wherever they were headed, I wasn't going to catch them. Without radar, I couldn't track them and, without cause, Miami-Dade would not interfere.

Bobbing in the last of the larger boat's wake, I picked up my phone and pressed send. When the call went to voicemail, I wasn't really disappointed, having already decided I'd had enough for one day. I wanted to go home. She was probably still in the autopsy and, using that for an excuse, I left a goodnight message and headed south. I needed time to process what I had seen and would have to deal with Grace and Martinez in the morning. First, I needed a good night's sleep and to throw a few flies to clear my head.

Running the bay at night was getting to be routine. At first, I had been intimidated, but I knew the water now and my only fear was striking a submerged object. As I accelerated past the last marker small wind waves slammed against the low freeboard of the bay boat and I had to slow after taking some spray off the port bow. This kind of boat was the right choice for these waters, except for when a northeast wind was blowing across the open water. In that direction there were no barrier islands to block the weather like they did the typical southeasterly winds.

The extended ride gave me time to think and I started fitting the pieces of the puzzle together. I liked patterns and used the metaphor of a jigsaw puzzle to fill in the missing pieces. First you need to find the corners: motive, means, and opportunity are taught as the ability of the perpetrator to commit the crime. Without any of them, there is no crime. There is also an unknown element to most crimes—that is the human condition that motivates someone to pull a trigger or, in this case, strangle their victim. Motive is the reason and can fester for years. There has to be an event to force it to the surface. Jealousy certainly qualified.

The clock was ticking on Signing Day. All the recruits now aboard the *Temptress* would be surrounded by family, friends, coaches, and the local media—and in a few days they would all have signed their letter of intent. When it was over, the schools would be ranked by the quality of their recruiting class—and the boosters, for better or worse, would be judged by the results. This was Alex's entire year wrapped into a week.

Alex and Donna appeared united. Unless there was something below the surface, the couple was aligned in their motives which were to keep Rosen happy by recruiting the best high school athletes. The couple had an additional bonus, if they could keep them in step during their college years, the recruits might sign on with them as agents if they were good enough to go pro.

I understood the dockmaster's resentments, but pushed too far, could he kill? I wasn't even sure if he had been at the scene. I thought about asking Justine about the prints that she had found. It's not like he was the only one with a possible motive—the players themselves were often trouble. This was their one chance and each might do whatever it took to succeed. Right now, that seemed the most likely angle.

The dock lights guided me in the last quarter mile to Adams Key, and a few minutes later, when I was fifty feet away from the concrete, I dropped the engine into neutral. Setting out the fenders, I watched the drift of the boat. It had taken me a long few months to get it right and now docking was as easy as parking a car—as long as I figured it out ahead of time. Every approach was different because of the wind, tide, and current. Tonight, I had the benefit of the island to block the wind and the tide was slack providing very little current. After I readied the lines, I idled to the dock, cutting power at the last second before turning the wheel hard to starboard and letting the momentum of the boat finish the job. I sat there for a second after securing the lines, waiting for the island's alarm. I always judged my success by Zero's reaction. With no lights on at Becky and Ray's house, I suspected that he was snoring louder than the boat's motor and had missed the opportunity. I retrieved my gun belt from the waterproof compartment that I kept it in, when on the water, and stepped up on the dock. With no sign of Zero, I walked down the path, turning to the right at the fork and heading to my park service house.

When I went to get a beer from the refrigerator, I noticed the empty shelves. I would have to make the trek to the grocery store if I wanted to eat tomorrow. Living out here, there was no 7-Eleven on the corner. Provisions had to be planned. I sat at the breakfast bar and opened my laptop. There would be a strong outgoing tide in the morning and there was a channel I wanted to check out. I made a deal with myself that if I went through the pictures tonight I could fish in the morning. I loaded the shots I had taken earlier into the computer, and with a split screen showing the partiers on one side, I opened a browser window with the top recruiting picks on the other. One at a time, I went through the pictures and compared them to the profile images of the top hundred high school players. It was easy to identify most, with the current trend toward unique hairstyles: designs, dreadlocks and bleached tips were all the rage in the pros and the high-school players were quick to copy. I found all of them and noted names and hometowns. I didn't know how deep the colleges recruited, but figured if you weren't on the website you didn't matter to the Alexes of the world. If you were on his radar, you already had your ticket punched, it was just a matter of destination. All these kids had something to lose.

14

I had expected a terse email from Martinez sitting in my inbox when I woke. If my truck and phone had told him I was at Justine's in Miami, he would have called. Instead, I found a bit of civility in my inbox. There was no mention of my whereabouts yesterday or the murder at the club. He had either had a golf date or knew it had nothing to do with him or the park.

With Susan reassigned, I was all he had, and he was forced to work with me. That earned me a little respect, but also more work. Fortunately, he knew if paperwork was added to my workload, it would never get done, at least not to his satisfaction. He had taken some of that burden on himself, including writing my patrol schedules, something I had skirted before.

The email had a request for me to head to the northern edge of the park and have a look at Stiltsville. The old water-bound neighborhood of stilt-houses built a mile offshore and over the shallows on either side of Biscayne Channel were a thorn in his side and I suspected he had gotten a report of some nefarious activity in one of the remaining houses. What had once been a thirty-structure outlaw community built over the flats south of Key Biscayne had now eroded to seven. The fate of the area had been on the table for years, and finally, in the late seventies, the park's boundaries were redrawn to include the community.

The fight had continued, but subsequent storms and the wear and tear of being on the water was doing the work for the politicians. This was one of my least favorite assignments—the only area where I wore my gun belt. With plenty of concealment, it was the bad neighborhood of the park.

Just as I was about to close the screen, another email popped up. My heart leapt into my throat when I read the successful outcome of the request for a custody hearing. My attorney, Daniel J. Viscount, had done what he claimed only *he* could accomplish. There were strict instructions that I was to meet him at the county courthouse on Flagler at three o'clock tomorrow afternoon. It, of course, ended with a demand, stated as a request, that I should bring his fee. I shot off a reply in the affirmative that I would be there and, with a smile on my face, I got ready to head out to Stiltsville. The patrol did offer a few perks. Hiding in the pilings and shade from the houses lurked some pretty nice sized mangrove snapper and I looked forward to filling my freezer. Instead of the fly rod, I grabbed a pair of spinning rods and loaded them onto the boat.

"Heading to Stiltsville?" Roy's head popped up from his center console.

Zero was snoozing on the warm concrete, but when he heard my voice, he rose, shook off the sleep, and waddled toward me. "Yeah, might as well fill the freezer if I have to do that patrol."

"Careful out there. Your boy Martinez sent me a request to check out number seven. Said there was some vandalism reported."

I patted my pistol. He knew the area as well. "You want to run out together?"

"Sorry, my schedule's full today. Snapper bites pretty good though." He went to his console and removed something. "Hold up," he said, handing me two small packages. "Sabiki rigs. Add a weight to the end and cast 'em toward the pilings. Baitfish take'm like candy."

"Cool," I said, taking the packages from him and releasing the lines. I stuffed them into one of my cargo pockets that already had a

Ziploc baggie full of tackle. I waved at him as I pushed away from the dock and, turning to port, headed through Cesar Creek. I chose the outside route to save time and avoid the Featherbed Banks that ran across the inside passage.

The short pass to the Atlantic had a strong and usually tricky current. I had both scolded and helped dozens of boaters off the surrounding flats. Today it was running stronger than usual and I gunned the throttle to give me enough speed to have adequate steerage. That was the mistake that the inexperienced boaters made. They tried to navigate the winding passage at low speeds, thinking it safer. With the current often exceeding five-knots, running at idle speed was like treading water, making the boaters victims of the turbulent water flowing through the pass.

I plowed through at twelve knots to overcome the incoming tide and followed the trail of green and red markers leading to deep water. Once clear of the flashing light, I turned to port and headed north. The wind had dropped overnight and the water had a light chop—perfect conditions for the small bay boat and good for fishing. I got the boat up on plane as the miles-long stretch of Elliot Key flew by to port, followed by the smaller Sands and Boca Chita Keys. Fowey Rocks Light soon rose from the water on my starboard side and I headed toward the first in the chain of steel lighthouses running down the length of the Keys, standing sentinel over the deadly offshore reef.

Once I passed the light, I cut into shallower water, using the skyline of Miami as a guide until the first of the structures came into view. I slowed, scanning the water for the green #1 piling that marked the entrance to Biscayne Channel. These were shoal-ridden waters and, though I could see the number seven structure, the channel was the only safe passage. I entered it and halfway through the pass, cut the engine to an idle and turned to port. Raising the tilt of the engine until it was barely sucking water, I proceeded across the flats to the buildings.

The structures were now in a trust that was responsible for the joint-custody agreement between the owners and the public. The homes were rented out for photo shoots and small conferences—aka parties. The problem was that unless there was a boat tied off, you never knew if they were occupied. We got notice when an official reservation was expected, but the buildings were magnets for all kinds of unauthorized activity, from portable meth labs to kids' hangouts.

The water was only several feet deep and crystal clear, making it easier to steer while looking over the side than using the depth finder. I made my way between two colorful buildings and headed toward the southernmost structure. Reaching it, I circled the house and tied off to one of the pilings.

I climbed up the ladder and reached the deck surrounding the structure. There was no evidence of any activity. The windows and doors were intact and, after trying the knob, I found it locked. I peered into the windows as I circled. There was no sign of any wrongdoing.

My mission accomplished, I started to the ladder and looking down into the water, saw a school of small baitfish circling a piling by the boat. I moved faster now and, after reaching the boat, pulled out the package that Ray had given me. After securing a weight to the end, I attached the small swivel to my spinning rod and pulled the line from the package. Two of the dozen brightly colored tiny hooks snagged my shirt and after freeing myself, I tossed the weight overboard and casted toward a piling several feet from the boat.

The weight took the line to the bottom and when it stopped, I closed the bail. With small jerks, I retrieved the jigs and suddenly felt a tug on the line. I reeled faster, feeling several more tugs as I retrieved the line. Three small baitfish came with it as I slung the weight over the gunwale. I tossed them into a bucket and threw the rig again. This time, knowing what to expect, I pulled in a half-dozen more. Sticking the hook in between one of the small fish's lips, I tossed the line toward the piling and soon had a nice snapper aboard. Several more followed—enough to hold me for a few weeks.

There was no need to communicate with Martinez. He already knew where I was, and would only expect to hear from me if there was something wrong. I had no ice, so I tossed a bucket of seawater into the cooler with the fish, threw the remaining baitfish back, and untied the line from the piling.

Idling away from the structure, I decided on a course between the closest two structures hoping that would be a clear path back to the channel. On my port side were two yellow and pink structures and to starboard, a plainer building with a mansard style roof. Passing between them, I scanned the water for the dangerous coral heads that were famous for gutting the hulls of unsuspecting boaters. Several were knocked over, the result of careless boaters trying to anchor here. Skirting them, I steered closer to the two structures and cut the wheel to make my turn when something caught my eye. On one of the pilings by the lower building was a piece of fabric.

15

It wasn't something that would typically even arouse my curiosity, except it was new looking and appeared to be a dead match to the pieces I had picked out of the mangroves on Adams Key. Hoping this was not going to play out like I thought, I idled the center console until the hull brushed against the barnacle covered piling. Martinez would have a fit that the newly repaired boat had suffered its first blemish and I should have dropped fenders and come in from the side, but my attention was riveted to the piece of floral print fabric waving like a distress signal in the light breeze.

It was pinched between a sliver of the piling that had peeled back and I left it in place to preserve it if this was, as I suspected, a crime scene. Moving the boat past the piling, I took the time to drop the fenders, hoping to delay the inevitable, and tied off the boat. To one side was a ladder, installed to provide access from a boat to the house, was secured to the piling, and as I climbed to the weathered deck, I could see how the fabric had gotten there. I paused to look at it again before setting foot on the dock.

I had made enough noise that if someone were hiding inside they would know I was here. With my pistol held in front of me with both hands, I crossed to the one-story structure. The weathered siding snagged my shirt as I slid along the exterior of the building, and I had to pause to unhook myself before moving to the closest window. Maintenance was a never-ending issue here, part of the reason Martinez was lobbying for the structures to be removed.

With large windows on all four sides of the building, the room was well illuminated and I had no problem seeing the interior. The older, rustic furniture was askew. Several of the dining room chairs along with the sofa and a recliner were upended in the large open room. To the side was a kitchen with a bar littered with red solo cups and empty liquor bottles. I could see most of the room and inhaled deeply when, despite the evidence of a party gone bad, there were no bodies. There were still the bedrooms to search, inaccessible from the dock.

Moving around to the door, I checked the handle and found it unlocked. Lifting the lever with the tip of my index finger to preserve any prints, I pushed the door open and entered the room. Swinging the pistol from side to side, I cleared the main room and the bathroom. There were two more doors, both closed, off a short hallway. So far, there had been no sign of foul play, but as I kicked open the first door, the smell of death hit me.

Before looking for the source, I cleared the other room and, finding nothing living other than a couple of small crabs, I holstered my weapon and pulled the mag light from my webbed belt. Back in the first bedroom, I moved carefully to the bed, watching where I stepped so as not to compromise any evidence. The sheets were tossed to the side and there was a blood trail leading to the far corner. I moved around the bed and, there on the floor, huddled in a ball was a girl.

Between the smell and the pool of blood around her, I gagged and went back through the living room to the deck. Backup was at least a half-hour away, probably more. I would have plenty of time to collect myself and have another look. There was no doubt that she was dead.

I called Martinez first. Misty had been found in the park and she was alive. After she had run off, she was out of my jurisdiction. The dead body lying on the floor in the room between the wood-framed walls and me was clearly inside the park. He didn't like it, but I could hear the, "at least it's in Stiltsville," tone in his voice. He grudgingly acknowledged that this one was not going to be pawned off on Miami-Dade. My next call was to Grace Herrera. I would have loved to make amends with Justine by giving her the scoop on the dead body, but I had to follow procedure. She took down the GPS coordinates and said she would assemble the troops.

I had some time and texted Justine. There was no response so I suspected that she was out training on her paddleboard. I would have to deal with the day shift crew and Vance would probably be the Medical Examiner. I had no problem with any of them, I was just more comfortable with Justine and Sid.

With my calls made, I knew it was time to go back inside before the cavalry showed up. Once they got here, I would be in charge, but still pushed to the side—at least until the body was released by the ME and the forensics bagged and tagged. Taking a deep breath, I pulled out my phone, pressed the camera icon, and went back inside.

Moving slowly now, I worked my way around the perimeter of the main room. There would be plenty of fingerprints and evidence gathered later, but this was my one chance to try to reenact what had happened here.

From a quick count of the cups lying on the bar top and floor, I guessed that at least two-dozen people had been here. Thinking back to being nearly overrun by the *Temptress* last night, that was about the number of partiers that were aboard.

I could guess the drinkers had been young from the empty bottles; vodka and fruit-flavored sodas seemed to be the drink of choice. Aside from looking like a pack of high school football players had run through it, I didn't see anything else in the main room. I took only a cursory glance inside the bathroom, noting that at least one person had tossed their stomach into the toilet. I guessed that if I looked, signs of several more would probably be on the dock from those that chummed the fish.

The empty bedroom had been used and I found a bra and panties tossed to the floor. Without touching them, I confirmed that they weren't torn. At least whatever had happened might have been consensual. I heard the sound of a boat approaching and looked out the window to see one of Miami-Dade's police boats coming in hot.

Taking another deep breath, I entered the bedroom. This was a different scene than the first room. I could only imagine what had happened here. When I had looked earlier, I had focused on the body, now I scanned the rest of the room. The sheets were torn off the bed in the direction of the body. There was blood sprayed across the everything in its path. The pattern reminded me of the VIP room at the club. My stomach turned at what I suspected I would see if I took a closer look at the girl.

There was no choice. I looked out the window and saw the boat had pulled up to the dock. I would only have a few undisturbed moments before Miami-Dade descended on the crime scene. Moving around the bed, dodging what looked like an access hatch to underneath the house and being careful where I stepped, I squatted down to look at the girl. A floral print dress lay in a pile across the floor that looked like the same material as the piece I had seen on the piling outside the house—I had no doubt it had been ripped from the girl's body.

A noise from behind pulled my attention away from the body.

"This how you found her?" Grace asked.

"Yeah, haven't touched anything."

"What brought you out here?"

"Martinez asked me to patrol out here today. Just a coincidence."

"Funny how they seem to find you." It was Grace's partner.

Before I could respond, I heard Vance's voice. The hipster wannabe fly fisherman had been after me to take him out and I remembered Chico saying that the bite was hot now. I only hoped, if he asked, it would be out of earshot of Dick Tracy. Now that the Medical Examiner was here, it was his scene until he released the body and I stepped back to allow him to proceed. I wanted to move away, already knowing what had happened, but I remained glued to the spot. I felt someone behind me and turned to see that it was Grace.

Calling over to one of the techs working the room, Vance asked them to take pictures before moving the body. Once it was photographed from all angles, the CSIs stood and nodded to him. Slowly, he extended the girl's legs and eased her into a prone position. The only thing that saved me was what I guessed was the day-old crime. The blood had dried and the girl's skin had taken on a pearly texture that had no resemblance of life.

From where I stood, across the room, several things were clear. Grace and I started a running dialogue under our breaths as Vance dictated the same facts to his assistant.

"Bruises are pre-mortem," Grace started. "We'll need a rape kit."

I guessed that was only for the DNA. There was no doubt from the signs of struggle and the abuse to the girl's body that if there had been penetration, it hadn't been consensual. "Maybe they'll get something from her fingernails."

"Probably. Looks like your girl is going to have a busy night."

Vance probed the girl's liver, concluding as I had that the murder happened last night. He paused to calculate the time of death and came up with midnight—about an hour after the *Temptress* had passed me.

It was becoming clear now. Stiltsville had been built to avoid the eyes and ears of the law. My guess was that Alex and Donna, in order to keep the party going, had moved it here. His instructions to the dockmaster had probably been to stay out all night, but the party had gotten out of hand. I thought back to the other girl I had seen last night with makeup hiding the bruises on her face. I had actually been relieved to see her, hoping it was the girl from the beach. If I had found my two live girls, now I had to figure out who the dead one was.

"Bag her up. I'm done for now," Vance said. He rose and turned to me. "I guess this one's yours. Want to join me for the autopsy?"

I didn't, but there was something I needed to know. "Can you hold on a minute before you bag her?"

Vance nodded to his assistant and the deputy stopped.

"Just a minute." I left the room and, avoiding the numbered cards placed by the other investigators, walked out the open door, down the dock, and hopped onto my boat. From the watertight compartment I removed the medallion I had bought yesterday, put it in my pocket, and went back inside.

"Here," I handed the chain to Vance.

"What's this?"

"Try it on for the murder weapon."

He gave me a strange look and we all moved to the body. Leaning over, he held the chain a few inches from the dead girl's neck. "Could be, but where'd you get it?"

"This one's just a knockoff I bought at a souvenir store. Alex has the real one."

"I'll get a subpoena and have it collected," Grace said.

"Let's hold off on that. That chain's been handled by at least two dozen people." I pulled my phone out and showed her the pictures and described the party I had seen last night. One clearly showed the group of boys dancing around with what looked to be the murder weapon.

When Vance and the body left, everyone except the techs quickly followed. I took off as well and started constructing a timeline on my way back to Adams Key. I wasn't done for the day, but my uniform was. It was a brief stop, except when Zero alerted Becky that I was there.

"That bitch stole my dang phone."

"I'm sorry about that. I didn't catch her in time," I started to explain, trying to think of an easy way to tell her where it was. "She tossed it."

"You got it, right? All my baby pictures and whatnot are on it," she said.

"It's in the bottom of the bay. I'm really sorry, but I'll help you get them from the Cloud and see if Martinez will replace it." We both knew he wouldn't. His issues with me were minor compared to Ray. In charge of maintenance on the islands, he was always needing money to keep the buildings and campgrounds maintained in an environment that did all it could to reclaim them.

"Shoot. I got the Cloud thing. See what you can do with the boss."

I thought I had gotten off easy and took the opportunity to head over to my house for a quick shower and change of clothes. Cleaned up, I packed an overnight bag to replenish what I had used from the drawer at Justine's apartment. It was one thing to use the space, but we weren't far enough along to ask her to do my laundry.

Taking a quick look to see if Becky was still following me, I went for the boat and managed to toss the lines and idle into the channel before Zero found me.

16

It had been just past noon when I'd left the murder site in Stiltsville. Now, with the sun dropping in the sky, I headed across the bay to Bayfront Park and the inevitable interrogation by Martinez—all so that I could have use of the truck. I knew there was little chance of getting by him and his cameras.

The murder scene was etched in my brain making it hard to think about anything else until I remembered the snapper in the cooler. Becky had distracted me and I had forgotten that it was still aboard. In typical park service fashion, the cooler was an older Igloo. Actually, until the start of the Yeti craze, the Styrofoam encased plastic had been the standard for years—the only issue was that they weren't very effective, especially in the South Florida heat and humidity.

Not wanting to waste my catch, I pulled across to the pier at Bayfront Park and tied off, then walked over to the bait and tackle store to buy some ice. Several minutes later I was back aboard. After draining the now bloody water I had added earlier I dumped half a bucket of fresh seawater in the cooler, opened the two ten-pound bags and poured their contents over the water and fish. The iced seawater would make a slurry, partially freezing the fish.

As I lifted the last fish and placed it in the brine a gaggle of brightly-colored kayaks slid past and I heard a voice that chilled me more than the ice.

"Fishing on duty again, Agent Hunter?"

I looked over and saw the stone-faced Susan McLeash. They hadn't taken away her special-agent uniform, which was still too tight in the wrong places, but at least some of it was covered by a bulky PFD. Underneath a wide-brimmed hat, she smiled at me, and before I could react, reached into a watertight hatch, removed her phone, and took a picture. They would surely be on Martinez's desktop before I docked and walked upstairs.

Cursing my luck, I slid the fish below the ice, closed the lid and threw off the lines. The park's dock was just around a bend in the mangroves and a minute later, I was tied off in my slip. Grabbing my phone, I checked the screen and saw a message from Justine. After pecking out a quick update, I headed toward the entrance.

Mariposa was both friend and ally. From the reception desk, she called over and greeted me. It'd been a few weeks since I had finally succumbed to her dinner invitation and she was after me for another date. It had been fun, until Justine and I were called away by none other than Susan. I still had the taste of her husband's Appleton 21, the rum only allowed for guests. I knew he would be eager for another dinner, if for no other reason than he could drink it.

"I'll check with Justine when I see her later," I answered before she could ask.

"Better go see the boss. He's been asking for you."

I thought of Susan and the fish. "There're some snapper in the fish box of the boat. Why don't you take them. The ice'll hold them till five, but I'm not thinking I can get back out to the island until much later. She thanked me and I headed upstairs.

I would have preferred a full-frontal assault, but per usual, he kept me waiting while he was on some kind of urgent phone call. While I stood there, I noticed a shiny new trophy on his shelf. I privately theorized that both the calls and trophies were props. Otherwise, this was not business as usual. After waving me to a chair, which was in itself unusual as he typically left me standing, he sighed and looked me in the eye.

"This is complicated," he said.

His world was black and white or he made it appear that way. Things either were, or weren't in his budget or on his spreadsheets. I had a feeling I knew where he was going with this, and let him continue.

"Stiltsville has been a thorn in my side since the last hurricane." He placed his hands together on the desk and sighed again. "Depends which way the wind is blowing as to whether it's going to stay or go, but either way, it's on our turf and our responsibility. Damned bastards in that trust think we should be the ones maintaining and renovating the structures. I'd be happy if they were gone for good."

I listened to his rant and, on this rare occasion, agreed with him. Especially after what I had found this morning, it would be better if the old houses turned into reefs.

"I'm guessing it was a pretty bad scene," he said.

Martinez was in a benevolent mood. It took all of ten seconds to figure out why after I noticed he was dressed in his podium uniform. I guessed the news about the murder had been released and he'd made the morning news. I took the opportunity to ask for a replacement for Becky's phone and was surprised when he didn't turn me down cold. Ray cost him a lot of money, but the guy was irreplaceable, and if he wanted him to live out on the island, he knew he had better keep his wife happy.

Whatever his goal, it was working in my favor. I pulled out my phone, opened the pictures app, and handed it to him. I watched as he scrolled through the dozen or so pictures I had taken.

"Well done, Hunter."

The pictures, now in the Cloud with everything else on my phone, would of course be leaked anonymously to the news. There was going to be a press conference in time for the six o'clock news and the crime scene would provide another reason to eliminate the water-bound neighborhood. "I was going to head up to Miami to check the forensics."

"Yeah, sure," he said, turning to his twin monitors and dismissing me.

I walked into the hall thinking something was missing. He hadn't mentioned the fish or Susan. Even though he was happy now, he would never have given me a pass. That meant that Susan hadn't told him—yet.

As I drove north I thought about what I had seen last night. With just a few days to go until the signing deadline, there had been enough testosterone running around Pier 4 to fuel a moon shot. I thought about Allie, who was just a few years younger than the players, and couldn't help but think about how far off the rails we had gone raising our kids. Living in California had given me a front-row seat to the damage helicopter parents and an entitlement society could do to them. I pulled into the marina and parked. Walking across the parking lot, I tried to breathe deeply and calm myself, but every third or fourth breath, I felt a tightness in my chest that told me I was still feeling the adrenaline from the crime scene and not in control of my emotions.

Assuming it was the same person that killed both the girl and the club manager, it was their connection that would solve the case. Any of those recruits I had seen on the deck of the *Temptress* last night had the means and opportunity to rape and murder the girl. They all had the strength, had been out at the house, and had access to the Turnover Chain.

Three hours after I had left Stiltsville, I walked toward the locked gate and found the dock deserted except for a man dressed in khakis and a work shirt hosing down the deck of one of the boats.

With no one in sight, I walked over to the dockmaster's office. The man cleaning the boat had given me an idea and I wanted some more information on the day-to-day workings of the marina. The high school boy must have still been in class and an attractive twenty-something came to the counter when I walked in. She wasn't blinged out like the boy had been, but her jewelry told me she was making more than the IRS knew about.

"Hey, Kurt Hunter from the National Park Service," I said, holding out a card. I purposefully omitted the Special Agent title.

"Dawn," she said, taking the card and thumbing it with her finger. "What can I do for you?"

She was clearly impatient, and I guessed that uniforms were not good for tips. I glanced around the room and found what I was looking for. "You have surveillance video from Tuesday night?"

"We respect our yacht owner's privacy here. You'll need a warrant."

I had no doubt they tipped well for such protection. "No worries. Quite the party last night," I said.

"Wasn't here," she said, probably upset that she was off and had missed out on the tip money. "Is there anything else?"

"Any idea where Alex and the recruits are?" I asked, figuring I might as well take a shot as long as I was here.

"A bus pulled up an hour or so ago and they all loaded up."

"Know where they were headed?"

"Not a clue."

"Thanks for your help," I said, walking toward the door.

"Hey," she called out. "Did one of them kill that girl?"

I wondered how she knew and then heard the static and someone call for the Miami Beach Marina on the VHF radio. I'm sure there had been some radio traffic after I called the murder in. I turned back to the counter.

"I can't comment. You know, ongoing investigation and all," I paused, "unless you have some information."

"Alex and Donna are alright, but some of those boys are trouble."

I already knew that, but she was talking so I indulged her.

"I guess some of them have been groomed for this. They're not really grounded in reality."

I had a festering feeling that the killer, though probably not a sociopath, had an altered version of how life worked. He had probably never had a girl say no to him.

"My high school boyfriend was one of those idiots. Tore his knee up in the State Championship and that ended everything—including us."

She looked like the ex-cheerleader type. "Yeah, I guess this signing day is pretty important to them." I leaned on the counter. We were buddies now.

"It's all they have." She shrugged.

This was getting too sentimental. "Any chance I can get out on the dock and have a look around?" I asked, changing the subject. I could tell she was about to say no. "The other dockmaster let me out there."

"He probably shouldn't have. Getting my kid brother a job has turned out to be more trouble than it's worth."

The difference was clear in how they handled themselves. Dawn made her tips from being discreet and helping the yacht owners maintain their privacy. She was also more careful of how she displayed the gains from her efforts. Her brother was the opposite. He would have sold out any one of them to the highest bidder. I thanked her and walked back to Pier 4.

17

Making sense out of what was going on in my head was going to require some thinking time. There was no running off to fish today, so I went with my next best choice and called Justine.

I got the okay to come on by with the caveat that she was pretty busy. A jolt of guilt shot through me when I realized that I had my own work to do and needed her resources. Pulling out of the marina, I hoped that she was working on the forensics for the dead girl. Justine had cut her own deal and worked with a degree of anonymity that the day crew didn't have. They were more of a team, working together in the newly renovated upstairs lab. Justine had been a hold-out, liking the night shift and preferring to work alone. She had held onto her own office and smaller lab downstairs. It was an arrangement she liked, but it was coming to an end.

The pre-rush hour traffic was mind numbing. Crawling along the 836 at fifteen miles per hour, I put my right foot on auto-pilot and tried to prioritize what my next move should be. I was still going under the assumption that the same person committed both murders. It was a likely scenario at this point, but until the actual Turnover Chain was found, whatever similarities I had demonstrated with the souvenir store replica were purely theoretical.

Alex would have been a convenient fit and he had been my first suspect, but the evidence was steering itself away from him. He had no reason to kill either the club manager or the girl. His success depended on recruiting players. Both were needed for his business plan. Ditto for Donna. I didn't like either of them, but as they say: "the facts are the facts".

These were crimes of passion, and both looked more like someone unable to handle their emotions than a premeditated murder. That in itself pointed to a younger person. This moved the compass to the players who would do whatever it took to get the scholarship as a stepping-stone to the NFL.

The dockmaster, Kyler, was also interesting. I had seen his immaturity on display last night and he too was fighting for his education, except he would be earning his way. Losing the lucrative tips at the docks would likely put an end to that dream.

By the time I arrived at the crime lab, I was as confused as when I had left the marina. Hoping Justine could pull me out of my funk, I entered the building and headed downstairs to her lab.

As always, I couldn't help but watch her from the hallway through the glass window. Her back was to me. The lab coat swayed gently, brushing against her hips as she moved to the beat of the music in her headphones. She liked it loud and I entered the room, hoping to sneak up on her.

"Hey!"

I had no idea how she knew I was standing there. "Hey!" I tentatively moved close to her, hoping for a kiss. She leaned over and pecked me on the cheek and I almost melted when her eyes locked onto mine and she smiled. Mariposa was right on with her after-action analysis of our dinner—the girl had my number.

"What are you working on?"

"Some gang thing from Liberty City. I think the brass is onto us." She smiled. "It was a good run."

I had suspected this might happen. More often than not, we had ended up working together and several of those cases had placed Justine in a compromising position. Some of this might be payback for the rumored fraternization, but we had discussed this at length. I worked for the feds and she for the locals. That was a pretty far cry from interdepartmental relations. Even so, I knew of several detectives, Grace's partner included, who would have liked to see the end of our relationship.

"Too bad."

"Well, the good news is that it's not pressing. I can be out of here in an hour or so."

I hoped that was an invitation. "I can stay busy," I said, sitting behind one of a pair of computer stations on a high desk by the wall. "Can you log me in?"

"Sure thing, lover boy," she said.

As she reached past me, I could feel the curves and heat of her body. She lingered a few seconds longer than it took to enter her password. Maybe her boss taking her off the case would have a positive impact on our relationship. Glancing back at her as she walked to her station, I watched as she put on her headphones and started moving to the barely audible reggae beat. I turned away before she caught me looking.

With my attention focused back on the monitor, I entered the 247 website for the high school recruiting rankings. I had a dozen names from my research last night and now it was time for some old-fashioned police work. One at a time, I dove into their bios. I was a longtime football fan and had always respected the better coaches, knowing that preparation was the missing link in many programs. It was interesting looking at the players from a coach's perspective. I was fascinated by the success of Bill Walsh's 49ers, Belichick's Patriots, Saban's Crimson Tide, and Urban Meyer, wherever he ended up. I dared not say the last name out loud after he was labeled a traitor for leaving Florida.

These programs focused on the system and found players through the draft, free agency, or recruitment. They often passed on talent, as star players often came with baggage and issues. The Heisman locker room was littered with past winners who had failed, not because of talent, but because of what was in their heads. Unfortunately, The U, fit into the latter category.

I tried to look at each player through the coaches' eyes. If I were in charge of handing out scholarships, half would be instantly eliminated. It was these castoffs that I focused my attention on. Dequan Johnson, Billie Smith-Jensen, and Reggie Willis were the standouts from this group. Each were five-star, first-team all-American players, but train wrecks off the field. I focused on their antics.

With the help of Justine's password, I was able to go where many coaches could not and I entered each player's name in the database that the police used to track minors' arrests. Adult arrest records were in the public domain. Minors' were protected and their records were often expunged when they turned eighteen. On my phone, I pulled up a picture of each person from the party last night as I looked at their records. Between these and the headshots in the recruiting page, I hoped to get an idea of what made them tick.

After reading the juvenile arrest records of Billie and Dequan, I cut Reggie from the lineup. What I found was a phenomenon that I had observed in other cases. I had learned to look to the edges of the sample you were studying. The middle would be average. Even for top-level athletes, average meant they probably stayed within the lines and played by the rules. Successful programs were built around the average player, complementing them with elite athletes only when they fit the mold.

Dequan was the cream of the class; one of the top five recruits in the country. Billie was in the bottom ten percent of the top hundred. No small accomplishment there, but still not average. It was these two who had the most to lose or gain on signing day. Now, I needed to figure out if either was desperate enough to commit murder. I left the juvenile records database and did a search for University of Miami football recruiting.

I found what I was looking for on Facebook. On a booster-sponsored page, the activities for the athletes were listed. There were several events where the booster with the right "level" of contributions met the players. Tomorrow morning was such an opportunity. A meet and greet was scheduled after a combine-type practice where the assistant coaches would evaluate the players in speed, strength, and agility. I wasn't a booster, but I'd be there as well.

"Done," Justine said, startling me.

"Sorry, I was a little wrapped up."

"Getting anywhere?"

"Just wondering how far I should go in trusting my instincts."

She reached over for me. "I think they're pretty good."

When she kissed me, she must have seen the face on the screen of my phone. Dequan Johnson stared back at her. "That one of those recruits? He looks like the U-type."

I let the comment go, but couldn't help but think that she had confirmed my intuition. "It's pretty early for us. Want to grab a bite to eat?"

"Sure. Whatcha got in mind?" She took off her lab coat and hung it on a hook next to the door.

I instantly regretted not asking if we could just go back to her place and almost changed course. "Maybe that taco place down by the water?" We both preferred a good dive bar to a four-star restaurant.

"That'll work. Want to leave the truck here and ride together?"

I looked at her again and decided I wasn't letting her out of my sight tonight. Whatever friction had been between us earlier was gone. I'd still better figure it out, but if we were good now, I wasn't fighting it. "Sure."

We headed east toward the MacArthur Causeway. "Not much traffic on the 836 tonight," I observed.

"Dude, we gotta talk about this 'the' thing. People can tell you're a California boy right off, adding 'the' to the road names. If they wanted to call it *the* 836, they would have called it *The* 836." She smiled and winked. "Got it?"

"Roger that." She was right, and the last thing you wanted if you were stationed in Biscayne National Park and dealing with the homegrown Floridians from Miami-Dade was to be labeled a Californian.

Instead of following 836 to South Beach, Justine turned south onto I-95 for two exits and headed toward the Miami River. We drove well inland from the towering hotels and condos downtown by Brickell Ave where the river meets the bay. The buildings here were lower and older. Justine pulled into a strip center with the river running behind it.

Even though the water was all connected and Adams Key was only about fifteen miles away as the seagull flew, it was different here. For starters, the river was darker, even during the day, from the industrial runoff and rain. Water quality was a problem in Miami, but the only way to cure it was to stop development, and that wasn't happening anytime soon.

We entered the small restaurant and were greeted by the owner. He led us back through a pair of open sliding glass doors to a narrow deck on the water. Margaritas were delivered with a bowl of chips and a green salsa. Our schedules didn't allow many date nights and these moments were special.

We both ordered the fish tacos and, while we waited, I sipped the top shelf drink and watched Justine. She seemed truly happy and I silently promised her more of this. All work and no play had ruined my marriage; now it looked to be the cause of the friction between us. We sat sipping our drinks.

Before our dinner came, Justine excused herself to use the restroom. I looked over the water, thinking life was pretty good, when I heard her call my name from inside the restaurant.

18

I found Justine by the bar, staring at the TV. "That's one of those guys you were looking at."

I asked the bartender to turn up the sound and we stood there watching Dequan Johnson being led off in handcuffs. I immediately recognized the smug look on Dick Tracy's face as he pressed down on the boy's bleach-tipped dreadlocks and pushed him into the back seat of the cruiser. I got a little satisfaction when he wiped his greasy hands on his uniform pants. The door closed and the camera panned to the newscaster holding a microphone in front of Grace Herrera. She was giving the typical canned response, essentially revealing nothing other than the arrest was being made in connection with the murder at the club.

"Is this connected to the murder out in Stiltsville?" One of the reporters thrust a microphone in her face.

She hesitated and I wondered how much the media knew. The murder was no secret; it had been broadcast over the VHF and Miami-Dade's network. Anyone with a scanner could have picked up the call. My question was answered when the several pictures I had taken earlier appeared on the screen.

Grace pushed away the microphone and ducked into the car. Interview over.

"Figures," I cursed under my breath.

"What?" Justine asked.

"Martinez posted those from my phone." I already knew everything on my phone was uploaded to the National Park Service's cloud. Martinez had used the technology to his advantage.

"Why would he do that?" Justine asked.

By now, we had relocated to two seats at the bar. The server had brought our drinks and chips and our fish tacos soon arrived. I pushed my empty drink toward the bartender. "He wants Stiltsville gone. More bad than good happens out there. The maintenance is also a drain on our resources." I paused thinking I was sounding like my boss. "I have to say after being out there today, I agree. The buildings are in bad shape. I think he's hoping the exposure of the murder along with the pictures of the trashed house will help his cause."

"He's probably right," she said.

The mood from earlier was broken. We sat in silence, watching the news and eating our tacos. Once again, work had intruded on our relationship. There was only one thing that could make this worse, and when my phone vibrated on the old galvanized metal bar top, I glanced a the sceen. It was Grace Herrera.

Justine saw it, too, and I shrugged at her, stood, and took the phone out to the deck. I wasn't trying to be secretive; it was just loud in the bar.

"Congrats on the arrest. Saw you got Dequan for the club," I said, leaning on the railing and looking out over the dark water.

"A witness came forward."

I wouldn't put it past one of these kids to throw another under the bus to gain an advantage. They might have been partying together, but they were more rivals than friends. Many had competed against each other in high school and now they were vying for a limited number of scholarships. You get anything on Stiltsville?" With the forensics tech sitting at the bar, I already knew most of the answer.

"We're still waiting on the forensics."

I had a feeling they weren't going to get what she wanted. "Why didn't you call me?"

The line went silent for a minute. "We got some pressure from upstairs to make an arrest."

"So, you arrested him for the murder at the club to keep it in your jurisdiction. If he's good for both murders, you get all the credit."

"That's why I wanted to talk to you. It's not my decision."

I disconnected without saying goodbye. Looking out at the water, I watched a barge being pushed by a tugboat downriver. It was kind of how I felt, being shoved around by forces working their own agendas in the background.

"Hey," Justine said, sliding up next to me.

"Hey." I explained how I got pushed out of the case. "Now that they have him for the strip club murder, it'll be easy to just add another charge on. Miami-Dade clears their books and gets the credit for both cases."

"Unless it's not him," Justine said.

I turned to look at her.

"There's still a water cooler in the crime lab, it's just upstairs now. Just because I like my little hole downstairs doesn't mean I don't talk to the day shift."

"And they've got nothing on the club?" I knew a single eyewitness was not going to make the DA happy.

"*Nada.* There's so much evidence it'll take forever to sort it out. Those prints are going to get more hits than the girls that were there. I don't think that room has ever been cleaned."

"But there's a ton of forensics out in Stiltsville, including DNA from the rape kit. They're banking on that showing it's Dequan; case closed."

"Exactly. But that's gonna take a while. Wanna go have a look?"

As badly as I wanted to, I paused to be damned sure I wasn't going to get her in trouble, or screw up our relationship. "I was kind of looking forward to something else."

"True that, but the night is young."

It was just after eleven, maybe early for her, but it was late for me. "Are you going to get in trouble?"

"Sid called earlier. I was going to put him off until tomorrow, but it's still technically my shift until two. Just doing my job sir."

I badly wanted revenge on Miami-Dade and agreed. We went back inside, paid the check, and were back on the road. When we passed the turnoff for her apartment, I looked down the road at the palm trees and landscaping illuminated in the dark night, wondering if we were doing the right thing.

"He said to come by," Justine said after talking to Sid.

"Did he say what he wants?"

"Nope, things are never that easy with him and it's on the way."

She turned off the highway and headed for the Medical Examiner's offices hidden in the shadows of Jackson Memorial Highway. Parking by the back entrance, next to one of the vans, we left the truck and walked up the loading ramp to the door. Justine pushed the intercom button while I stared through the safety glass at the sterile hallway.

Sid buzzed us in and I followed Justine to his office. He sat behind his desk, looking at something on his computer.

"Whatcha got, old man," Justine asked as we entered. She went over and pecked him on the cheek.

I hung back slightly. He had asked to see her, not me. "Come in, Detective."

I let the title go, actually preferring it to Special Agent. "Hey, Sid."

"How's the fishing?"

It was his typical greeting. "Got on a couple of snapper and found this one." He didn't care much about the fishing; it was more about the dead bodies I had found in the process.

"Come look at this. I think I can save your stomachs and just show you the pictures."

I silently thanked him for that, and we slid around to see what he was looking at. I almost turned away when I saw the blood, but Justine moved closer.

"Vance ditched me for another case and left me with the autopsy of the body you found this morning."

"Did you do the rape kit?" I asked.

He peered over his reading glasses at me, telling me without moving his lips the question was unnecessary. "Yes, and yes, she was raped—but you can tell by the bruising that it may have been as long as twenty-four hours prior to the murder."

I suspected it was the night before when I had found Misty on Adams Key. Those girls were running from something. "Can you tell how much before?"

"Not exactly. They're pretty close in time, but the bruising is fully developed, something that takes about a day."

"Want me to run the DNA?" Justine asked.

He handed her a sealed evidence envelope and a clipboard which Justine signed and handed back to him creating the chain of evidence the prosecutors would need if the case went to trial. "I think Miami-Dade got the wrong one," he said.

He had experience, but I didn't think he was clairvoyant. "How can you tell?"

His tired brown eyes studied me again, asking how I could be so stupid. I was trying his patience and searched for the answer before he said it. I wasn't sure if it was the late hour, or the two margaritas, but I was having trouble piecing this together.

With an excuse to go back to the lab, we left his office feeling like the gang of three again. Our little group: a park service agent, an almost retired night-time coroner, and a basement-dwelling forensics tech had done more to solve several other cases than the entire police force. Walking to the elevator, I felt my energy coming back; having a chip on your shoulder had that effect.

Back in Justine's office, we stared at each other, not really sure where to begin. "The DNA?"

"Yeah that, but gonna take some time to get the results. There's got to be something else. Let's take a walk and see what the other half has been up to."

She led me upstairs to the main lab. I already knew that Justine preferred to use the old lab rather than the newly remodeled one. The cavernous room was filled with gleaming stainless steel. Hundreds of LED indicator lights on the equipment made the room intimidating. "I feel like we shouldn't be here," I said, looking around the dark lab.

"Want me to issue you a secret agent badge?" Justine said, moving to the locked evidence cabinet.

Instead of the welded steel grates used in her office, this one had smoked Plexiglas doors. She punched a code into the backlit keypad to the side and the electronic lock buzzed. The doors opened slowly followed by a blast of cool air. I looked around for the telltale stainless-steel drawers, but instead found only cabinets. Justine worked through them, reading the labels until she found what she was looking for and opened it.

The expected alarm bells never sounded. She removed the box and we left the room. "Why the chill in there? I was half expecting dead bodies?"

"They go for the dramatic up here. One of the reasons that I like my cave." She led me to an empty table and set the box down. "This is the evidence collected from the club. Might as well start here and see if they have anything on DeQuan.

We went through the box full of clear envelopes, careful not to break any seals as we held the contents to the light. Justine had collected these samples and knew what she was looking for. One of the last envelopes had a small stone in it. Under the light I could see it was a diamond. "I found some blood on this. Find the setting it goes in and we've got the murderer."

I took the envelope and held it under the light. The small diamond shimmered back at me, and I had an idea where I might find its owner.

19

"You're looking at that like you know who it belongs to," Justine said.

"Can you tell if it's real?"

"Sure, forensics 101."

She took the envelope and signed the front before slicing it open. We moved to a microscope sitting next to several large-screen displays, which lit up when she pressed the space bar on the keyboard. "Nice stuff they've got up here," I said, while she positioned the stone on the glass below the lens. The equipment in the lab made what Justine worked with look like toy store seconds.

"I sneak up here sometimes, but generally I prefer the old-school stuff."

After pressing several keys, two of the monitors went black, leaving a fuzzy image of the stone on the one closest to us. She tapped out another sequence on the keyboard and the diamond came into focus. Even I knew real from fake and this was real. I couldn't tell the carats, but if my ex had gotten one that size in her engagement ring, we might still be married.

My stomach fluttered at the thought of my past life and the

hearing tomorrow. I still needed to transfer the five-figure sum for Daniel J. Viscount's retainer. "I forgot to tell you that I got a custody hearing tomorrow. That big-shot lawyer came through."

"That's awesome." She leaned into me. "I can't wait to meet her."

I smiled back and realized I now had something else to be nervous about. Getting my mind back on the case, I looked at the display, confident when I saw the pits and flaws that they meant the stone was real. "Pretty sure that's the real thing. Not a prize, but it probably goes for close to a grand."

"Whose is it? I don't think those recruits can afford that kind of bling—yet."

It wasn't ego that stopped me from speculating on who owned the diamond. We had been on enough cases together that she knew how I thought and that I wasn't scared to be wrong. "Where'd it come from?" I asked, trying to dodge her question.

"I pulled it out of the gash in the club manager's neck."

"It's too big for the Turnover Chain," I said, and took a breath before I threw my theory out there. "That dockmaster was wearing earrings. They looked like this could be a match for one of the stones."

"What's a dockmaster doing with this kind of bling?"

"Tips are good and he's been moonlighting for Alex." I explained what I had learned from his sister, my take after meeting him, and his unusual behavior on the dock last night. "He's obviously got some issues with these kids getting a free ride. There's also something between Misty and him. I'd bet he was the one driving the van."

"High school can be a hard deal. It's tough watching your peers, some of whom you know are not going to succeed, get all the attention," Justine said, turning away and resealing the evidence bag.

There was something in the way she said it that led me to believe she had first-hand knowledge. "He's a smart kid. There's some resentment going on here, but I think greed might be the bigger motive." I followed her back to the high-tech evidence locker. After returning the box to its shelf, we stood outside the doors.

"Check this out," Justine said, entering the code.

There was a small beep, followed by doors silently moving on their concealed hinges. Just when the doors were about to close, there was a hissing sound like a vacuum seal. "Cool, but not cheap." I wondered how Miami-Dade was going to pay for this, and thought about giving Martinez a heads up that he might want to pad his budget. I looked at my watch. "It looks like there's not much we can do until tomorrow."

"Works for me. Follow me home?"

"I'd follow you anywhere."

I thought there was a little more sway to her hips as she led me out of the lab; what you might call a bit of swagger if you were a Cane's fan. After locking the door, we went back downstairs to her lab. Austere would be the only word to describe it after the high-tech equipment in the new lab.

"It's going to be hard making the move upstairs."

She must have caught me looking around. I gave her a hug. I was sad, too. We'd had some special time here—just the two of us. I doubted it would be the same working upstairs. She grabbed her bag and we left the old lab. She flicked a switch and looked through the glass window in the hall as if she were looking at it for the last time. We stood there for a minute.

"I'm thinking of asking for a transfer," she said.

Change was okay, I told myself, hoping it wasn't going to require relocation. "Where?"

"FDLE. I'm tired of these Miami-Dade pricks."

I knew she was at least verbally abused by some of the detectives. She had reassured me it didn't go any further than good-natured ribbing, but I knew it was wearing on her. "Tampa?" This was their closest office and a five-hour drive.

"They're throwing around some feelers about opening an office in South Florida."

"That sounds promising," I said, exhaling the breath I had not realized I was holding. "They're supposed to be good to work for."

"Yeah," she said, turning away from the glass partition.

I followed her down the hall and upstairs. We left the building and went to our separate vehicles. Driving back to her apartment, I considered the bombshell that she'd just dropped and how it affected me—or if I should even be factored in her decision. I decided that it was not my place to influence her and vowed to only offer support. I did allow a caveat that I could cross my fingers when we spoke about it.

We drove back to her apartment. I thanked the gods for the wine that she offered and cursed myself for not buying any. Our moods soon returned to normal and we both fell into bed together. It was just before three and I knew I should close my eyes and go to sleep, but when Justine slid up next to me, that was the furthest thing from my mind.

EVEN WITH HER BLACKOUT BLINDS, there was no need for an alarm when I stayed here. If I didn't know better, I would have thought that Martinez had a sixth sense, though it had nothing to do with ESP— it was technology. He knew how to do three things with his computer prowess: track me, update his spreadsheets, and make it appear the he was a busy man through CCs and BCCs on his email. I felt Justine kick off the covers next to me and I reluctantly answered.

"Can't get enough of Miami, Hunter?"

I knew he was baiting me. "Got a lead on the Stiltsville case."

"I saw your buddy Grace Herrera locked up one of those recruits last night. Looks like it's back to patrol for you."

I knew where he was going. If there was to be no glory for him, there was no case for me. "I think they've got the wrong guy."

"Oh, and you know better?"

This was turning into a pissing match I didn't want to get into. I needed a closer, something that would look good for the park service as well as work toward his personal agenda. "I've got some forensic evidence and a theory that Dequan was set up." My theory was a little half-baked but had percolated overnight. It might not pan out, but if I could match the diamond found at the club, I could keep the case open. His silence was my permission to continue. "If we keep this investigation open, Miami-Dade loses face and Stiltsville remains closed as a crime scene."

"Make it happen," he said and disconnected.

I knew his response was a temporary reprieve—probably just for today. And standing in front of me was my first decision. I realized there must be something wrong with me when Justine came out of the bathroom and moved toward the bed, and I considered getting up. Fortunately, I came to my senses.

After showering together, I went to my drawer and pulled out shorts and a dress T-shirt. I smiled when I looked at my stuff. I quickly stuffed the newly granted space with a clean uniform, a few pairs of shorts, and a couple of T-shirts. Granting her the same space at my house was easier and she had half the dresser.

It was a half-hour later when we were having coffee, that I asked her to come with me. If I was on a short leash, having the world's best forensic tech tagging along would hardly hurt; and I needed her on my arm where we were going.

"Look at you in your civvies," she said.

"Got plans?"

"Nope. I've been training pretty hard. Could use a day off. Whatcha got in mind?"

"Recruits are doing an open combine type day out at the U. Any interest?"

"Back to the old alma mater. Sure, as long as you don't break out that stupid chain."

I wasn't going to make that promise. "Let's get some breakfast and head out."

We took Justine's car. If I was going in plain clothes, I didn't want the park service truck to give me away. I was also hoping the switch was going to send Martinez for his antacids. Justine, knowing the area a lot better than I did, drove.

We passed through Coconut Grove and entered Coral Gables. The practice facilities were on the south end of campus off South

Dixie Highway by Red Road. The parking lot was about half full and several news vans were near the entrance. We parked near the back and walked hand in hand toward the gates. When we entered the practice field, I was in for a surprise.

I'd had a mediocre high school football career in a small town in Northern California where other things were more important. But from Texas down through Louisiana, Mississippi, Alabama, Georgia, and Florida, football was everything. The recruits had been issued Hurricane practice gear and were working their way through the same drills run on every field in America. I knew them well enough to jump in if I had to. What I immediately noticed was the level that these kids were on. They were bigger, faster, and better than anything I had ever seen at this age. The arrogance and cockiness, with the exception of a couple of players, Billie being one, was gone; there was work going on here.

We strolled in front of the low bleachers as if we belonged and I studied the crowd. I found what I was looking for near the fifty-yard line. Dressed in full Cane's swag, Alex had attached himself to two other coaches like a remora sucking up to a shark. He was deep in conversation, pointing to one of the players running pass patterns with a small group of receivers. I recognized the one he was pointing at from the docks the other night.

"That's Billie Smith-Jensen. One of the guys he's recruiting."

There were no tickets or restrictions for the practice. It was coaches and players only on the field, but the sidelines looked like open territory. I led Justine close enough to where Alex was holding court to see and hear what was going on, but at the same time, tried to stay obscured by the bleachers. I happened to look back and saw Donna in the stands, sitting with several women who looked like the recruits' mothers. Our eyes caught and held for just a second too long—she had remembered me. I glanced back, trying not to stare, but she was looking right at me holding her phone to her ear.

From where we stood, Alex was only about five yards away and I could hear his phone ring. Donna was clearly warning him and I had to decide whether we should stand our ground or head out before he saw me. I felt Justine squeeze my hand, sensing something was up.

"Dequan would have caught that no problem. This legal crap is temporary," Alex told the coach before pulling the phone from his pocket. "I can assure you of that."

20

We ducked deeper into the framework of the bleachers using the slatted aluminum seats to cover our exit. I didn't expect any trouble, but neither did I want Alex to see us. Though Donna would confirm I was there, he was so focused on the field, I doubted that he'd remember unless he saw me with his own eyes.

We made our way back to Justine's car and left the facility. "We need to call Grace and let her know Dequan was set up. Alex is trying to use the arrest and his sway here to limit his options. The other schools won't touch him with this hanging over his head."

"You better refine your theory first. Once he's released, it'll be on the news and the real killer will get a heads-up."

I knew she was right, but the thought of a high school kid sitting in jail, thinking his dreams had ended before they began, turned my stomach. "Let's go find the real killer then."

"Okay . . . "

My watch said it was just before noon and there would be a few hours of school left. "Can we go by your office?" I had an idea of how to confirm the dockmaster was our man.

"I'm off today and that new lab is creeping me out. What do you need?"

"Just a computer monitor that we can use to blow up a few pictures."

"We're just as close to your headquarters."

The second-hand monitor passed down to me sitting on the desk in my office wasn't big enough, but I knew where the perfect one was. There was just one problem. I picked up the phone and pressed the button for the reception desk at headquarters. Mariposa answered.

"Hey, Kurt. Boss is looking for you, but I guess that's nothing new. Without Susan around, he's a bigger pain. I guess she did serve a purpose after all."

If that were all she did, I'd come babysit him. "He around?"

"He's upstairs. I can hear him pacing."

She couldn't, but I got the message. "We'll be there in about twenty minutes."

"We?"

"I've got Justine with me." Justine waved from the driver seat. I declined to pass along the gesture and disconnected. For the next twenty minutes, Justine drove while I formulated my plan and decided what I'd tell my boss. The answer was—as little as possible.

We had just reached the headquarters building and were walking toward the entrance when a gust of wind came across the water from the north, taking me by surprise. On a typical day, the first thing I did after getting out of bed was to check the weather. My job depended on learning to read between the lines of the forecast, something I had refined working out west. There, the problem was snow. The last thing you wanted was to be caught out on a foot patrol with a storm blowing in. They called it Sierra Cement and the heavy, moisture-laden snow brought in from the Pacific accumulated fast. Thunderstorms and squalls were the problem here and could come out of nowhere with little warning. I looked over the water at the hazy skyline of Miami where the wind was blowing and wondered if it were an omen. Dark clouds were gathering on the horizon and the first white caps had started to form on the bay. The weather gods were about to go to war.

"Looks bad," Justine said.

As a paddler, she knew how to read weather and water as well as I did. It was one thing to be caught in a twenty-foot boat, another on a paddleboard. At less than thirty inches wide and twelve and a half feet long, the dimensions were similar in scale to a toothpick. "Yeah," I responded and held the door for her. Mariposa came out from behind her fortress and gave her a big hug, which was returned enthusiastically. They'd only met once, but there was a connection there—probably at my expense. Mariposa motioned me upstairs with her eyes, dismissing me.

I had my phone in hand, ready to make this as short as possible and entered Martinez's office without the standard wait while he finished his latest urgent phone call.

"Decided to come to work Hunter?" he asked.

I sat across from him and looked at the empty seat usually reserved for Susan McLeash. I almost asked if she was guiding a tour this afternoon, worried that she didn't have the sense to check the weather. Instead of asking Martinez, I decided to check with Mariposa on the way out. It wasn't her safety I was concerned with, but her tour group. My boss stared at me across his empty desk. Handing him the phone, I asked him to pull up the images from the dock party.

"Got all that," he said, leaving the phone on the desk. He turned to the space where his dual monitors had sat.

Apparently, they'd had a baby and there was a third now. I immediately named it Susan. I couldn't help but look up at his shelf of generic golf trophies, wondering if the same thing had happened. Within a few seconds, he had the pictures up and spread across the screens. I moved closer, leaning over the desk. "That one," I said, pointing to the kid at the helm of the *Temptress*. "Can you blow up the head?"

Martinez manipulated a few buttons and the face of Kyler, the dockmaster filled the screen. It was his right side, and I could see the earring clearly. It held a diamond the size of the one taken from the club manager's neck. I needed to see the other side. "We need a better angle?"

Martinez scrolled through the pictures. There was one that just had the back of his head, but nothing of the left side. I sat there for a second wondering what my next move was going to be when a familiar voice blasted through the speakers of the VHF base station on the back of his desk. I cringed—it was Susan.

"We've got a mayday situation out here," Susan's voice echoed through the room.

I'd seen first responders in action and had accumulated enough training in my years with the parks service to qualify as one. From what I'd seen, there were good and bad ones. Martinez was instantly out of his element

I looked at him and he nodded. Walking around his desk, I took the microphone off the stand. "This is Special Agent Hunter. Please state your situation and position." Despite being on a first name basis with Susan, I used my title for the benefit of any of the tour group listening.

"We're about a half-mile south of Boca Chita. Big swells and a headwind. Can't go forward and too far to go back."

After almost a year here, having learned the ins and outs of the park, I instantly understood where the group was and how they had gotten there. It had been through fishing that I had learned the nooks and crannies of the miles of shoreline surrounding the park. Things tended to happen in what I call transitional space. In the forest, with a hundred thousand acres of land and just a few streams running through it, most of the action had been near water. Biscayne National Park was the reverse, and here it was the land that mattered.

"Hold on for instructions. We'll get help on the way." I released the talk button and looked at Martinez. "She must have gone out from the campground at Elliot Key and hugged the shoreline, but there's nothing but mangroves there. Nowhere to land." I saw the look on his face. He had no idea what to do. "What have we got for assets?" I figured he'd know the answer to that.

"Got your boat and Susan's. Ray's out at Stiltsville cleaning up that mess from the crime scene. "

"That's it?"

"You know the budget constraints we're under."

It was his answer for everything. "Call the Coast Guard. I'll see what I can do." I moved to the window behind his desk that overlooked the small park service marina while he called the Coast Guard. Sitting side by side were Susan's and my twin center consoles. At twenty-two feet, they could get there, but the groups generally ran between eight and twelve people. It would take both boats to rescue them. I already knew he was going to insist on us saving the kayaks as well.

Johnny Wells's thirty-nine-foot Interceptor was gone from its slip. I would call him and see where he was, but the ICE crew generally spent their days further offshore. The FWC inflatable was next to my boat and I reached for my phone to call Pete Robinson. Inflatable was the wrong word for the thirty-foot, soft-sided boat. It could hold the entire group and the twin Yamaha 250s would get us there quickly. His call as usual went to voicemail.

"Coast Guard says they have two situations already with the storm coming up. They'll be an hour," Martinez said.

"You coming, Hunter?" Susan's voice blared over the speaker.

We didn't have an hour with her in charge. A bead of sweat dropped from Martinez's brow and I looked at his face. He was out of his depth. This was mine to handle. "It's going to take both boats. Justine's downstairs—she can take one and I'll take the other. Stay tight with the Coasties and call Johnny Wells with ICE." I gave the orders and left before he could comment. Taking the stairs two at a time on my way out, I called Ray's cellphone. I knew his radio was probably off and he had a policy about answering his phone when Martinez called—voicemail.

"Wassup, boy? Get on them snapper I told you about?"

"Hey. Got a couple. Listen, it's gone to hell here and I need your help." I explained the situation and he agreed to leave Stiltsville to meet us. He sounded grateful for the distraction.

"He go off on you or what?" Justine asked.

"We've got an emergency. Martinez can barely find his way from the green to the next Tee box. I need your help."

"I'm here for you, Kemo sabe."

"Whatever I can do from here," Mariposa said.

I gave her the same directions I had given Martinez and asked her to keep an eye on him. At least I could count on her to do what I asked. "I need the keys to Susan's boat."

Mariposa reached below the desk and tossed me the key tied to a floating chain formed to look like big red lips. "She gave me a gas receipt before she got kicked down the dock. Should be ready to go."

"Why her boat?" Justine asked as she followed me out the door.

"We're going to need both. Can you handle hers?"

"You bet."

I tossed her the key as we split up, each taking the finger pier to our respective boats. Having only four lines out, I was first to leave the slip and idled into the turning basin while Justine untied the half-dozen lines Susan had used. Within a few seconds, we were both idling out of the channel.

I had a few minutes until we reached the end of the channel and thought about Dequan. Grace should know and I pulled out my phone to fill her in, but the call went to voicemail. I left a brief message, thinking that at least I'd done what I could, and turned my attention to the boat traffic.

Several boats were cruising in, running faster than the *idle speed* only zone, totally disregarding the park service boats as they tried to reach the safety of their trailers before the storm hit in earnest.

Ignoring them, I picked up speed and after passing the last marker, turned toward the northeast, and pushed down on the throttle. Checking every minute or so to make sure Justine was still behind me, I crossed on the port side of the #2 marker for the Turkey Point Channel and corrected course for the barely visible lighthouse rising just above the landmass of Boca Chita Key.

From the look of the whitecaps, the wind was blowing at twenty knots and the seas were building. I worked the trim tabs and the engine tilt, but it was impossible to get enough speed for the hull to plane out. Barreling forward at twelve knots with the bow jutting out of the air and guzzling gas was not the ideal way to travel, but heading into the three-foot waves, we had no choice.

21

I saw them bobbing in the waves just beyond the point at the end of Sands Key. The group was dangerously close to Lewis Cut, a narrow and dangerous pass leading to the open waters of the Atlantic. Susan's mistakes were compounding. First, she should have cancelled the trip, or changed the plan to remain in protected waters. Second, she was going the wrong way. If she had taken a moment to figure out the wind and current, she might have realized that if she rafted the kayaks together, they would be pushed right into Sand Key. Instead, she had decided to plow forward and try to reach Boca Chita Key and the promised destination. From where the group was, the lighthouse seemed much closer, but they were fighting the wind and seas. With an inexperienced group, in the park service's sit-on-top kayaks, they would never reach it. At least she had called for help.

The group was paddling hard, but getting nowhere, and the tug of the outgoing tide through Lewis Cut was just about to grab ahold of them. I slowed to figure out a plan, but decided the only thing we could do was to round them up like sheepdogs and tow them to safety. Justine had slowed and was matching my course and speed about eighty feet off my starboard side. It was too far to yell across the water, but anything closer would risk a collision. "Save yourself first" was rule number one in the rescue books. You couldn't help anyone if you were in trouble yourself. I held the VHF microphone up for her to see.

"We need to get them over to the leeward side of Sand Key," I spoke into the mic. I was using channel sixteen, the general hailing and distress channel that was monitored by the Coast Guard, FWC, and ICE. I also knew Martinez would hear us.

"I count eight kayaks. We can split them," Justine responded.

I needed to confirm that this was the whole group. "Headquarters, do you copy?"

"Here, Agent Hunter," Martinez's voice squeaked back.

"Can you verify that there are eight kayaks in the group."

He dropped out of the conversation and I continued to outline my plan with Justine. It sounded easier than it was, especially with Susan as an unknown. The wind would surely be a problem, having a greater effect on the larger center-consoles than on the kayaks. We agreed and I started idling upwind toward the group.

"Hunter!" Susan hailed over the VHF.

It wasn't hard to tell from the tone of her voice that she was out of control. I'd seen her make bad decisions in other situations, usually using subterfuge or excessive force to try and gain an advantage. Neither of her typical tactics was going to work here. "Roger, we are moving in to rescue," I responded.

"What the hell are you going to do?" she screamed.

One of my former rescue instructors had told a story of how he'd had to knock one of his victims out in order to save them. I wondered if I could do this with Susan. It would certainly be easier to handle the group without her. "Coming around upwind. We'll meet in the cut and let the wind move us toward you."

"Then what?"

I had to calm her down and giving her a task was the best way. "Do you have a tow rope?" The hundred-foot line should have been standard equipment.

"That thing in the bag?"

"Yes. Pass it between your group, so you are rafted together."

"Okay, I'll try," she said.

Justine and I had completed our upwind run and were allowing the boats to drift back toward the kayaks. Fortunately, the cut was deep and we didn't have to worry about grounding. We kept our boats a safe distance apart as we let the wind bring us toward the group. I could see them clearly now. Susan was fumbling with the tow rope. At least she was busy. When we were within earshot, I called out and told them our plan.

Trailing our dock lines behind us, Justine took one side and I took the other. Within a few minutes, we each had a string of four kayaks behind our boats. Instinctively, I counted and wondered why Martinez hadn't gotten back to me with confirmation that this was the entire group. It didn't matter right now as we towed the kayaks to the cover of a small mangrove-lined cove that was protected from the wind. The water quickly turned from green to brown, and I moved as close to the shore as I could before dropping the Power-Pole to anchor the boat. Looking across, I saw Justine do the same. I had been so busy with the "rescue" that I hadn't noticed the weather had passed. The entire incident could have been avoided if Susan had done her homework and kept her head. I had to decide whether to allow them to continue or pull the plug. After looking over at Susan, I chose the latter.

One at a time, we both pulled in the kayaks and loaded the passengers into the center consoles. I had three already in my boat when I looked at the last kayak behind me. It was Susan, and I had an impulse to release her, but I saw her tear streaked makeup and hauled her aboard. There was nothing to do but feel sorry for her.

"Now what? This is quite the mess. We have to get the kayaks back too, you know," she said.

It had been a mistake to fight back that impulse. "People first," I responded calmly. "Was your group eight?" I still had not gotten confirmation we had everyone.

"Yes, including me."

"Okay. We'll load them half and half."

"Right, I'll take one group on my boat and you and your girlfriend can take the other," Susan said.

She liked to be in charge, and I figured at least now that everyone was safe, it would be okay to let her have her way and save a little face. We were about to split the groups when my phone rang. I glanced at the display and saw it was Grace. "Hold on, I need to take this," I said turning away.

"Your message was pretty vague," Grace started.

"Sorry about that, we had an emergency out here. I wanted to give you a heads-up before I left."

"Well, I did what you asked and told the prosecutor not to proceed based on some information that you have. I've kind of stuck my neck out here without knowing why."

"I owe you an explanation, but I've got a group of paddlers I have to get back to headquarters."

"We can only hold him another few hours before we either have to formally charge him or release him. Someone paid for a top-notch lawyer," she paused. "Name's Rosen. If he gets wind of this, the boy's gonna be on the streets."

"Rosen is a big-time booster. He owns a handful of yachts over at the Miami Beach Marina," I turned back to find Susan and Justine yelling at each other. "I gotta go. I'll call as soon as I get back to headquarters. Just hang onto him for now. If I'm right, the real killer will get wind of it and might do something stupid."

She agreed, though I knew she was powerless to do anything except relay the message. For now, I had a catfight to break up. Before I could figure out what Susan was up to, we all turned when we heard a boat coming toward us. It was up on plane, running with the waves, and I could see the bow pointed in our direction. Once past the point of Boca Chita Key, the forest green fabric on the T-top came into view. Ray dropped to an idle while well offshore so as not to swamp the kayaks with his wake, and idled toward us.

"Got 'em all?" he called out.

"Yeah, all good."

"Cool. I saw a boat out at Stiltsville tied off to one of those houses. I thought they pulled the plug on rentals after the murder?"

"Me, too." Martinez had been behind that move. It was something I should probably check on. "Hey, can you help take these guys back, so Justine and I can run out there and have a look?"

"No problem. Gotta pick up some ice anyway," he winked at me, telling me the snapper bite was still on.

That was the last thing on my mind now. I organized the group, sending three with Susan and the rest with Ray. Each boat had four kayaks attached to a towrope from its transom. Justine looked on with me as they pulled away.

"That woman's nothing but trouble."

It had taken a while for her to come around, but she had seen the light. "Mind if we run to Stiltsville?"

"That'd be cool. I've never been out there."

I waited a few more minutes, watching until I could just see the T-tops of the two park service boats on the horizon before pointing the bow north and idling away from the mangroves. Minutes later, we were past the Boca Chita Lighthouse heading toward the open bay waters. I decided to stay on the inside to allow the shoals on our starboard side to absorb the remnants of the storm. With the seas down, I pushed the throttle and the hull planed up on top of the water.

The black top of the Cape Florida lighthouse marking the southern tip of Key Biscayne came into view just before I saw the first roof of Stiltsville. To the west, I found the markers for the Biscayne Channel and circled around, staying in deep water until I was lined up between the pilings with the #20 and #21 placards. Cutting back to an idle, I saw the boat that Ray mentioned tied up to one of the structures.

It looked familiar and as I approached, I saw the name, which I remembered from the docks of the Miami Beach Marina. I pulled back on the throttle and let my boat drift. I was looking at one of Rosen's boats and the chances that this was an innocent visit diminished.

For once, I was certain that I was within my jurisdiction. Stiltsville was in my territory and this was suspicious activity. I had no reason or desire to call Martinez for permission. Backup might have been a good idea. I looked over at Justine. She had been around the tail end of several cases where things had gone sideways and I trusted her entirely—in fact, she had saved my life in one.

"That's one of the boats from the marina that belongs to that booster. This can't be good."

"Gee, here's a thought. Take cover behind one of those other buildings and call for backup."

It was a good idea and probably the right one. There was no indication anything untoward was happening, at least right now. It seemed it was already standard procedure for Alex to take recruits and his girls out here. "Okay, we'll duck behind that one." I motored over to one of the structures across the channel. The long low building offered both concealment and protection. I thought for a second about who to call. There was no sign of poaching, which would have been a call to the FWC. I was also starting to remove Pete Robinson, their local agent in charge, from my list. He rarely answered his phone. ICE had no jurisdiction in a local case, leaving me with my friends at Miami-Dade.

I pulled my phone from the watertight compartment below the helm and hit Grace Herrera's number. She answered right away.

"His lawyer got him out. I left you messages."

I took the phone from my ear and glanced at the screen. There were two voicemails and a text, all from her. "Okay, I was underway and had to stash the phone. I've got one of Rosen's boats out here in Stiltsville. Want to join the party?"

22

I wasn't sure what was going on in the house, but I knew one thing. My custody hearing was in a little over two hours—I had a problem. If I were to leave now, I could just make it to downtown Miami, where the case was scheduled to be heard. A suit would have been preferable to my shorts and T-shirt. At least if I had my khaki park service uniform, I would look like I came from work. A shower would also probably help my case. Neither was going to happen.

"How long until Miami-Dade gets here?" I asked Justine, who was listening to the police scanner through an app on her phone.

"Probably about twenty minutes. They have two boats coming out of Government Cut now."

I did the math in my head and it still worked. There were plenty of places to dock on the Miami River that would be walking—or running—distance to the courthouse on Flagler Street. "I need to take off as soon as they show. I have that custody hearing."

"How's that going to work out for you?" she asked, looking me up and down.

I ran my hands down the front of my shirt, in an attempt to smooth out the humidity induced wrinkles and shrugged. "It's all I got," I said, feeling a nervous flutter in my stomach. Custody battles are a bad deal, mostly on the children, but they take their toll on the parents as well. I had wanted to avoid court and figured, despite how much it hurt inside everyday when you think of your kids, that it was the best thing for our family. Despite everything that had happened, we were still that: three people forever tied together.

I checked my watch again and looked back to the west where I expected the cavalry to be coming from at any second. Several boats were making their way out to the reef, but there was no sign of Miami-Dade's finest. A sound came from the building and I turned my attention to the reason I was here.

A door slammed, and then there was the unmistakable sound of a gunshot. My last, best-case scenario for getting to court had now turned into the worst-case. There was every reason to believe that something bad was going on in that house. Since it was in my territory, I was in charge.

"You have a plan B?" Justine asked.

Scenarios had been running through my mind about how to deal with the present situation. I was conflicted between my duties as an officer and as a father. Being a parent was the easy choice and I had already decided to turn over the scene to Grace—until the gunshot.

"No," I admitted. Whoever was in the house was probably not aware that we were interested in them. Ray had already been out here in his park service boat and we were docked at the same structure across the channel from where the murder had taken place. The buildings were totally exposed. Whoever was inside could see for miles in every direction. There would be no stealth approach. An overwhelming show of force was probably the best option. It was going to take a concerted effort to take the house, and again, I thought about relinquishing control to Grace.

There was still no sign of backup and I leaned against the seat deep in thought.

"Call your lawyer," Justine said.

"Good idea." I pulled my phone from my pocket and searched my recent calls for his number. Hoping that I wouldn't need to know him long enough, I hadn't bothered to enter his name into my contacts.

Finding the only 305 area code without a name next to it, I pressed the *connect* button and waited, trying to figure out what to say.

"Hunter? Where are you. We were supposed to meet an hour before the hearing. Things are moving fast here."

It had to be this one time that the wheels of justice were turning quickly. "I'm involved in a hostage standoff out at Stiltsville."

"Don't they have SWAT for that?"

There was no way to explain the nuances of the situation now. "I'll be there as soon as backup shows."

"Hurry. If we miss the hearing, this is going to look bad. You do have my retainer…?"

Of course that was his concern. "Yes. I'll get back to you as soon as I'm on the way."

"I'll try to stall," he said.

Fortunately, the ticking clock in my head, counting my attorney's billable hours paused when I heard the sound of a boat approach. I'm sure Daniel J. Viscount was still billing, but at least I was distracted. I turned to the mainland, shielding my eyes against the sun. Its position in the sky reminded me again about the time.

"Whoever is in that house is going to know that we're on to them when police boats start circling," Justine said.

She was more focused than I was. I looked back at the house. "You're right. We need to look at this as a hostage situation." I knew from experience that using a cell phone on a boat running at full speed was futile so I picked up the microphone and hailed the approaching police boat on the VHF. My eyes shot to the roof of the house across the channel, remembering Martinez's base station in his office. There was no antenna and I could only hope that whoever was in there didn't have a handheld.

We agreed on a rendezvous behind the furthest building. At over a quarter-mile away, and obstructed by several other structures, I doubted whoever was inside could see us. Justine had heard the conversation and released the lines. A few minutes later, with a constant eye on the other building to see if we had been noticed, we pulled up behind the A-Frame house. Two other structures blocked a direct line of sight from the Hicks House where Rosen's boat was tied up.

"Whaddaya got, Ranger Rick?" Grace's partner started, as the police boat pulled up to the dock.

She threw him a look. "Hostage situation?"

I told her about the door slamming, the shouting, the gunshot, and that there had been no activity since.

"These old houses can play tricks on you," Dick Tracy said.

I ignored the comment. "How do you want to handle this?" I looked directly at Grace. I didn't want her partner's opinion.

"You want us to take it over?"

"They're your assets and I have to run."

"You have to what?" Dick snarled.

"Personal matter. This should be simple for you guys."

Grace talked to her partner for a minute. "Okay. If there was a gunshot, I'm calling in a SWAT team. We'll stand by until then."

"Thanks. This is important."

"You want to hang out, Doey? Could have some cleanup for you when this is over."

She dressed him down with her eyes. I knew she hated the nickname. Her last name was Doeszinski, but many had shortened it to Doey, or J. Doe. "We'll be back."

She sounded like the Terminator and he looked away. Grace was on the phone with her people, organizing whatever it was that the SWAT team needed. It was the best I could do under the circumstances, and I nodded to Justine to release the lines. Once we were free, I reversed the engine, barely missing a piling behind us, and jammed the throttle forward. The boat lunged, again just missing the Miami-Dade police boat. I breathed out after seeing that Dick Tracy hadn't noticed.

Pulling forward, I cut the wheel to starboard in order to make the wide turn into the channel when I heard another gunshot. This time, a woman's scream cut clearly through the humid air. I wasn't going anywhere. Justine must have seen the concern on my face.

"Call your lawyer and see if I can go."

Appearing in court on my behalf wasn't anything I would ever ask anyone. "You'd do that?"

"With SWAT coming out, I'll be on the sidelines here. If I'm needed, like he said, it'll be for cleanup and I don't have my equipment here."

"I can't ask you to do that."

"That was a direct order. Call him."

I dropped the transmission into neutral and looked around the scene, wondering if there was anything I could do. SWAT would be here shortly, and now that Grace and her partner had heard the gunshot for themselves, I'm sure they had called in air support as well. Martinez was not an issue. This was a fifty-fifty situation and, even if it went right, Miami-Dade would dominate the news coverage. The decision was mine and unless I was saving a life out here, my daughter came first.

I turned into the channel and pushed down the throttle.

"What are you doing?" Justine yelled over the roar of the engine.

"Going to court," I said with finality.

Once clear of the last marker, I turned to port and lined the bow up with the rise in the Rickenbacker Causeway. Beyond the bridge, I could see the skyline of downtown Miami and glanced down at the chart plotter to plan my approach to the Miami River. I felt Justine's hand on my back and felt good about my decision, even as three Miami-Dade police boats sped past.

I had to slow for their wakes and chanced a look back at Stiltsville. It was still quiet and I turned back to Miami, thinking about the hearing and rehearsing what I was going to say for the thousandth time. I had always thought my ex had overreacted, if there was such a thing when your house got firebombed, but the circumstances were unusual. There were tens of thousands of law enforcement officials in this country arresting people every day. The percentage of those targeted by the criminals they brought down was infinitesimal. In our case, it was the cartel flexing its muscles and making a statement, not something really directed at me or my family.

"Hey," Justine yelled.

I noticed the boat coming right at us and cut the wheel to port, barely missing the bridge piling. Gritting my teeth, I tried to focus. Returning to the channel, I lined up the marker indicating the mouth of the river and pressed down on the throttle. A quick glance at my watch told me I had just enough time to make the hearing. I was about to ask Justine to text my attorney when the static from the VHF stopped me. A voice I knew came through the speaker and hailed me.

"Hunter, we need you out here," Grace called out.

"Roger, can you give me details?"

"I'll call your cell."

I had to stop to take the call, but gathered from her need to speak privately that I had been wrong and whoever was out in that house was monitoring the VHF and knew SWAT was on their way. Seconds later, I saw the screen light up, showing Grace's name, and I answered before it rang.

"Things have gotten complicated," she started.

I could tell she was out of breath. "Go on," I said, placing the call on speaker so Justine could here.

"There're two of them, at least in the house. They must have seen the police boats heading out and they came outside. It looks like a high school age kid holding a gun to a girl's head."

"I can be back out in a few hours," I said, checking my watch again. There was no chance the hearing would go past five.

"Here's the thing. The guy holding the gun—he's asking for you."

23

"Why is he asking for you," Justine asked.

"Good question." I had nothing else to say, and a decision to make. "I interviewed him and I guess we connected." My second guess was that he thought I was somehow an inferior opponent compared to Miami-Dade, but I wasn't saying that out loud.

"And I thought it was just the hot chicks who connected with you. What are we going to do?"

We sat there in the middle of the bay, floating with the tide, as I tried to decide. I was pulled in both directions, and wondered if I should just let the tide make the decision for me. As I looked down at the water, I saw it was slack—no help there either. It finally came down to the hearing. It would be expensive and maybe count against me to have to reschedule, but I'm sure Daniel J. Viscount would be willing and able to make it happen for another five-figure check. I had raised Allie to be sensible and analytical. She was almost fifteen now and hopefully would understand why I missed the hearing.

"I could still go. Just drop me off," Justine broke the ice.

"Are you sure?"

"Just do it. Like I said before, I'll just be waiting around the crime scene until after whatever is going to happen happens."

My phone vibrated again and I looked at the screen. It was my attorney, and I looked at Justine, who reached over and pushed my hand forward on the throttle. I got the message, and we were quickly up on plane and heading straight for Dodge Island. I had docked on the backside of the cruise ship port many times, but today, I cut the wheel to port, steered around the western tip of the island, and entered the river.

We passed a small island with high-rise condos guarding the entrance and cruised past them. I didn't slow until I saw the first bridge ahead. Needing both land and water information, I had my eyes on the chartplotter; Justine's were on the map on her phone. Between us, we decided on the Riverwalk as a drop-off point.

Several commercial ships caused a small traffic jam in the narrow passage under the Brickell Avenue Bridge. I waited impatiently for them to pass. Once through, I pushed the boat forward and saw the railing for the Riverwalk just under the next bridge. Fighting the wakes from the two commercial vessels that had just passed, I tried to ease up to the seawall, but underestimated the current of the river and heard the crack of fiberglass against concrete, which was unfortunately not a new sound for me. The collision threw Justine, who was waiting in the bow off balance, and I thought for a second that I would be fishing her out of the river. Her agility overcame the collision. She easily grabbed the railing and hoisted herself over. Turning back, she gave me a thumbs-up before taking off down South Miami Avenue. The courthouse was about six blocks away on Flagler. I yelled after her something I thought I would never say to a woman again. She didn't look back, and I assumed it was lost in the humid air.

I had no time for a soliloquy as another wake tossed the bow of the boat within inches of the seawall. Justine was out of sight now. I backed away, spun the wheel, and headed toward open water. I glimpsed at my watch after passing under the bridge again. It was almost five. Hopefully, she would make it in time. For now, there was nothing else I could do and turned my attention to the channel markers.

Ignoring the idle speed warnings, I slammed down the throttle after passing under the last bridge and cruised back toward Stiltsville. Five o'clock signaled the return of the charter fishing fleet which resulted in a steady stream of large boats and their wakes to deal with. With no light bar and only the stenciled letters on the bow which were probably invisible to the captains perched several stories up on their flybridges, I was just another boat. One by one, the huge sportfishers cruised past me. Colorful flags with pictures of the fish they had caught flew from their outriggers and happy anglers clinked beer bottles in the spacious cockpits, all oblivious to my law enforcement standing. The small park service boat was tossed back and forth in their wakes. Refusing to succumb to the rough water, I plowed ahead. Every third or fourth wave, the propeller cavitated as the boat left the water and I braced myself for impact, waiting for the bone-jarring crash when the hull landed. Each collision threw seawater over the entire deck, including me.

Once I was drenched, it was cathartic and allowed me to focus on what I could control. I had to trust Justine and my attorney; there was nothing I could do on that front. What I could do was save a young woman's life and that path lay ahead.

Key Biscayne flew by on my port side as I headed toward the tiny structures on the horizon. The island acted like a funnel for the boat traffic coming into Miami. The pounding continued as I crossed the wakes left by fishermen and pleasure boaters making their way back from the offshore reefs and the Gulfstream.

Finally, I reached the channel and saw a cluster of Miami-Dade boats tied to a dock by one of the houses. I headed toward them and with the assistance of one of the deputies, tied off to one of their boats. I had to step up onto the gunwales of the center console and take another step to reach the higher Contender, which was at dock height. When I crossed to the dock, I saw a command center had been set up.

"Hunter," Grace called. "Over here." She waved me over.

"You the guy he's calling for?"

"I guess." The man had a worn-down look and appeared sullen under the weight of his captain's bars.

"Looks like a young kid. He's got at least a pistol which he was holding to the girl's head when he asked for you."

"I have no idea why he wants me."

"Doesn't matter. He wants you; he's got you. I've got a hostage negotiator here," he said, looking over at the structure adjacent to the house the couple was holed up in. "The officer here will run you over."

I felt like a pawn. There were at least twenty people, many in uniform, out here. They each seemed to know what they were doing, like this was all well rehearsed—which it probably was. A younger man in a uniform motioned me to one of their small craft, which I couldn't help but notice was bigger than mine. I put my boat envy on the back-burner and tried to focus on what lay ahead.

I had seen the look on the boy's face the other night. Jealousy tinged with rage was the emotion that came to mind. Though I didn't like him, I could sympathize, and did, which was probably why he had asked for me. The kid, though lucky that his sister had hooked him up with a good job, had worked for what he had. He was set to go to college in the fall on his own merits, not because he could play a sport that would enrich the school. When you looked at it that way, I could see his point. Why he had killed the club manager was something else, but he clearly had the character traits I had witnessed the other night. He was capable of it.

He had picked up Misty after her distress call. Maybe the murder at the club was an attempt to protect her. Misty was far from an innocent bystander. I had seen her in action. He was obviously infatuated with her—but would he kill for her?

If my theory was correct. He was guilty of assault and manslaughter, both a far cry from the well-oiled electric chair up in Stark. Maybe that would be an angle to diffuse this. With that in mind, I approached the small group set up across from the Hick's house. They were deep in conversation and I stood there for several seconds before one of them turned.

"You Hunter?"

"Yeah, what can I do to help?

The woman who appeared to be in charge approached. She stood with her hands on her hips as if she were evaluating me. Dressed in business clothes covered by a windbreaker with Miami-Dade SWAT on the back in bold letters, mirrored aviator sunglasses, and her hair covered by a ball cap it was hard to get a read on her, which was probably her goal. "Tell him you're here. That'll buy us some time." She handed me a megaphone.

I raised it to my mouth and before I could speak she shuttled me out the door. Now I felt less like a pawn and more like a target. I lifted the bullhorn again. "This is Special Agent Hunter." I looked at the woman for approval, but only got a tight-lipped nod. We waited.

"Dude, you gotta get me oughta here. This is all a mistake."

"Keep him talking," the woman whispered to me.

"I hear you, but first we need the gun." I raised my eyebrows and she nodded.

"No way. I want a fast boat that'll get me to the Bahamas—and some cash."

This was clearly not well thought out. He had probably grabbed Misty on a whim and taken her out here, thinking he had been found out when Dequan was released. Now he had gone too far and didn't know what to do. She likely thought she was being abducted.

"Send out the girl." I chose not to use her name.

"No way."

"This is going to end one way or another. You're a smart kid, you've watched enough crime stuff on TV to know how this is going to go down."

The negotiator gave me a scalding look. "You were supposed to buy us some time, not call him out."

It was quiet for a long minute.

"We need to take action. He has no idea what he wants and is likely going to do something stupid," the SWAT leader said. "I've seen enough of these to know this is going to end badly. There's no negotiating with someone that doesn't know what they want."

"What if I can get in there and disarm him?"

"Yeah right. There's no cover," one of the men said.

I looked around the structure. There would be no way to sneak up on him. That was until I remembered the floor hatch inside the house where the girl had been killed.

Installed for smuggling, the hatches were used to bring liquor and women into the houses and who knows what out. With the history of this neighborhood, I had to assume that each house had one. Crawfish Eddie's, The Calvert Club, and The Quarterdeck Club were three of the more famous places. In its prime, the neighborhood had twenty-one houses, all built to facilitate gambling and drinking during the end of prohibition. With the use of the hatches, sneaking things in or out of the exposed houses could be done in the dark of night.

"There're floor hatches inside," I said and outlined my plan.

The woman looked around at the three men with her.

"It's too quiet. We need to act," she said.

The three men nodded. It was all we had.

24

"I guess you have some idea about how we are going to get under the house without being seen?" the SWAT leader asked.

He had been called over to strategize, and was immediately my friend. I could tell he didn't like the negotiator. SWAT wanted action and my idea would provide that. "I'm thinking we create a diversion and I can swim up under there."

"You a good enough swimmer?"

I shrugged. "I'll get it done."

"You'll get it done with one of my men right with you."

"As long as he stays under the house. Hopefully we'll take him by surprise. If I appear through the floor, he knows me and might pause long enough for me to talk my way in."

"Your funeral. We can start circling the wagons here and bring in the perimeter. That'll get his attention and give you enough cover to get in the water. After that there's not much we can do. Sorry excuse for a target. Ideally, I'd set up a sniper on all approaches, but there's nowhere to stage them."

"If it makes you feel any better, he doesn't want to kill her."

"People do stupid things when they're under pressure."

He was right and I didn't see any other way. With SWAT, there was always gear involved and I was quickly provided a short wet suit, a mask, snorkel, fins, and a waterproof radio. My pistol was replaced by one of theirs that could withstand the water. I took a quick look at my phone to see if Justine had tried to reach me before moving to the far edge of the dock where I put on my fins and slipped into the water. My new partner, probably not too enthused about backing up a rookie, slid in next to me. We gave each other the thumbs-up sign and started swimming around the platform.

I could hear the activity on the dock above before we submerged. Orders were being given and the boats fired up their engines and started moving. Just before I dropped my head underwater, I thought I heard the thump thump thump of a helicopter. It was some relief that Miami-Dade was pulling out all the stops, but I knew this was going to end with me.

It was hard not to notice the beauty surrounding me as we swam around the pilings. The SWAT diver was in charge of navigation, so I followed him as we made our way around the house. Extended in his left hand was an underwater compass, which he checked at least twice a minute, easily changing our course by compensating with his kicks. It took me a few minutes to become comfortable with the gear. My snorkeling experience was limited, but I was a solid swimmer.

Below me, as if close enough to touch, were coral structures stacked on one another with small tropical fish swimming around them. I guessed at the brain corral for its resemblance to its namesake. The rest, I didn't know, but they were spectacular in shape and color. As my eyes adjusted to the diffused light, I could see larger fish in the slots of sandy bottom between the coral formations. I had to restrain myself from shooting to the surface when a large green eel appeared.

Around us I could hear the sound of the boats' engines. In my expedited dive briefing, I had been warned that the sounds coming from the surface and boats would be disorienting, but the captains knew where we were and I shouldn't worry about it. Despite the warning, the sound of propellers churning through the water was unnerving. It sounded like chain saws flying around me. Trying to slow my breath, I failed to put them from my mind. The only thing I did know was that once we were past the channel, the water was too shallow for them to follow.

We reached the deeper water and I had my first experience with current. Following the SWAT diver's lead, I adjusted my body position and kicked harder with my left foot. Seconds later we were across and I saw the same coral formations. The diver turned back to me and made a hand motion, which I assumed meant we were approaching the house. After another minute we were in its shadow and I could see the first pilings ahead.

Once we were underneath, the diver raised his head out of the water and started studying the structure above. It was a lattice work of beams, girders, and joists with what looked like a tongue and groove flooring system above. I noticed it was quiet now and wondered what was going on around us. The only thing we could do was keep to the plan and we swam between alternate sets of pilings looking up at the floor. I was starting to doubt myself when I saw a wooden ladder, or rather 2X4s nailed to a pile near the far side of the structure.

I motioned to the SWAT diver and together we swam toward them. Their condition was questionable, but above them was a hatch. We moved closer and I grabbed the bottom board. Slowly, I pulled my weight onto it to see if it would support me. It creaked but held and, one at a time, I removed my fins and handed them to the diver. Thankful for the booties, the SWAT commander had given me, I climbed up the rungs, carefully checking each one before I put my weight on them. One was loose and I almost lost my balance, but knowing it was just water below me gave me the freedom to push the limits of the old wood.

My hand hit the last rung and I contorted my body into a position to gain some leverage and push the door open. This was a big unknown in my plan as it easily could have been designed as a two-man operation and be locked from the inside. I hoped my instincts about smugglers were correct and they would avoid anything that would keep them from their destination. If the law were after them, they would want fast and easy access to the interior which had shelter and probably a cache of weapons.

Bringing myself back to the present, I studied the hatch. Something tapped my calf, causing me to almost lose my balance. It was the diver asking if I needed help. I shook my head and with the pistol now in hand, used my shoulder to press against the hatch. I was worried about the old rusty hinges creaking, but had put the cart before the horse. The hatch didn't budge. I looked down at the diver and shook my head. He reached down to his calf and handed me his dive knife.

The thick blade barely fit the moisture-swollen gap between the floorboards, and a fraction of an inch at a time, I slid the blade in until it met a resistance. When I could go no further, I pried on the handle. The blade was wide and thick enough that I didn't need to worry about breaking it, but the short shaft made getting leverage on it difficult. I looked around and saw an old piece of galvanized pipe hanging by one rusted strap beside the newer PVC piping installed to replace it. Pulling it loose, I placed the end over the handle of the blade and pulled down on the three-foot length of pipe.

Something moved and I froze. The next action needed to be planned carefully. I wasn't sure of the layout of the house and there was a chance the hatch would open within sight of the occupants. I tried to listen for any sign of what was going on inside, but between the boats moving around, the lapping of the water against the barnacle-covered pilings, and the thick southern yellow pine flooring, I couldn't hear anything.

Now, about to enter the unknown, I hedged my plan thinking two guns were better than one. "Let's go together," I said to the diver. He nodded and after dropping our gear into the water, he climbed up next to me. The gear was no longer an issue. We would be taken out by boat no matter how this ended. Perched together on the small board, we made a plan.

"On three," I called out. We both grabbed the pipe with one hand and our weapons with the other. "One...Two...Now!" There was no need for stealth, we needed speed. Together we pulled down on the pipe. At first the hatch resisted, but then gave way. The diver stuck his head through while I held the old wooden panel open. He scanned the room with his pistol and finding nothing, signaled back to me that the coast was clear. With the old wood on my shoulders, I stood, raising the hatch enough for him to crawl through. Once he was in the room, I followed and dropped the panel back in place.

We found ourselves alone in one of the bedrooms. While we were underneath the house, I had studied the plumbing and had a pretty good idea that the kitchen was on the far side of the house. Kyler and the girl would be somewhere in between.

Together we moved to the door. The diver turned the worn knob and gently pushed until a small crack appeared. I moved to his side and we both looked into the room. Sitting at the table to the side of the couch were Misty and the boy. They were in a heated conversation. I looked for the gun and saw it on the table about six inches from the boy's hand. Doubting he had the experience with the weapon or the sense to use it on Misty and create a standoff, I nodded to the diver.

We were in low crouches as we had been trained, but from this angle the couch blocked any view of the room. I stood and pushed the door just a little bit more. I should have known the saltwater would have corroded the little-used hinges, and they creaked.

He spun when he heard the sound and did exactly as I had predicted. In seconds, the gun was trained on us. Misty took the cue and ducked under the table, then crawled behind the kitchen island. With her safe, we had him outgunned two to one. It was time to start negotiating.

"Drop it and we'll talk," I said. "You're Kyler, right?" I said, trying to humanize the situation.

He nodded and glanced around, looking for Misty, but she was out of sight. I could see the fear in his eyes and his hand wavered as he wildly pointed the gun between us. I remembered the SWAT commander saying that anything could happen in one of these standoffs.

"Easy, I'm putting my gun down." I reached slowly to the floor, laid down the gun, and kicked it a few feet away. The movement created enough of a distraction for the diver to slide across the room and get a better angle on him.

I held my hands up and started talking. "What if I get the rest of the boats and helicopter out of here?"

"That's a start," he said.

"Okay," I nodded to the diver. With the gun still pointed Kyler's head, he raised the radio to his mouth and spoke to the commander. He nodded to me.

"They're going to pull back, but I need you to lower your weapon."

He hesitated a moment before placing it on his knee. "You going to listen to me now?"

"Let's get Misty out of the way first, then we'll figure this out." I didn't wait for a response. "Misty?"

"Over here. I'm alright."

Despite what she had put me through, I wasn't hardened enough not to care for her well being. "Why don't you go out the side door there and wait on the deck."

"Okay. What are you going to do about Creep Show over there?"

Kyler's face turned red and his hand went for the gun, but before he could raise it, the diver inched closer, making sure the boy saw him.

"Go," I yelled. "Now!" I watched as she stayed low and I just caught a glimpse of her on hands and knees as she crawled to the door, opened it, and went out.

"Billie did the whole deal." Kyler had dropped the gun and placed his head in his hands.

I recalled the bio of Billie Smith-Jensen: Defensive tackle from Venice, Louisiana. "Tell me," I said, moving to the table and sitting next to him.

25

THE WORDS POURED OUT OF HIS MOUTH LIKE A FLOOD TIDE THROUGH A narrow pass.

"Billie killed the club manager and the girl?"

This threw me for a loop; I had expected the case to be closed after a full confession from the kid. Now he was diverting the blame to someone else. "So why take Misty hostage and bring her out here?"

"I was trying to protect us. Billie was the one who beat them the other night on the boat. They jumped overboard because of him." He stared down at the floor.

I followed his gaze and saw the boat shoes. They had a ring of dried muck around them. Looking up, I saw he wasn't wearing earrings.

"And you grabbed the girl from the beach?"

"I was freaking out about Misty and I saw Heather. The players had calmed down by then, and I thought I was doing the right thing."

He probably had, not knowing Misty had found help and I was looking for her friend too. That solved the first mystery. "And the club? You were driving the van and both of you were at the club." The diver was getting antsy behind me. I knew Kyler should be in cuffs and on his way to booking. I was deviating from standard procedure, but it was my case, and if I had him talking, I wasn't going to stop.

"I was supposed to go pick them up and bring them back to the dock. Misty stayed in the van. When I got inside, I saw them harassing one of the girls, there were no bouncers there, so the manager tried to break it up." He looked up at me. "He grabbed Billie, who went into a rage and killed him. I tried to stop him and he went after me," he said, turning to show me a bruise on the left side of his neck.

That could explain the missing diamond. There was one more thing I had to know before we took him back to the mainland. "And what about the girl out here?"

"I couldn't stop him." He paused for a long minute to collect himself. "I asked Alex not to send me out alone with them. Most of the groups are different, kind of in awe at the whole thing. This one, with Billie leading them, was out of control."

That explained the fight with Alex at the dock the other night. I would let the DA get the rest of the story. I had learned enough, but there was one more question I needed an answer to. "Why would you help him?"

"I just wanted an in when I get to school. You know, things would go a lot smoother for a freshman that knew some players. If I turned him in, I would be an outcast."

The kid was a mess, but not a murderer and no longer a threat to anyone. I was getting anxious to end this and find out what happened in court. I needed to get back to my phone. "This is how it's going to go," I told him. "The officer there is going to tell everyone that we're coming out." I realized there were no handcuffs in either of our wetsuits. "You'll have your hands above your head and will leave them there until told otherwise."

"You're arresting me?" His eyes darted around the room.

"Let's just say we're taking you in for questioning." Unless Misty pressed charges, I didn't know what to charge him with. According to him, Billie had committed both murders. He could be involved as an accessory, or in covering them up, but if he came clean this quickly to me, I could only imagine what he would tell the DA if they offered him a deal to testify. I looked at the kid, almost feeling sorry for him. The cocky attitude was gone, replaced by pure fear. He was smart enough to know how much his future depended on what happened over the next few hours. "If I were you, I might call my parents and get a lawyer to meet you at the station."

I saw the conflict in his eyes between being a defiant teenager and a sensible adult. The conversation wouldn't be easy and I hoped he had the guts to make the call.

"Thanks." He seemed relieved.

"I need to get Misty off here first," I said, rising from the table. It was time to end this and find out what happened with Justine.

"Can I talk to her?"

I thought about that for a minute. "I think it's better if you don't. She's caused you enough trouble already." He dropped his head and I tried to remember if I had ever felt that way about a girl. "I'll talk to her." I turned to the diver and asked him to keep an eye on the kid. He nodded and I left the house.

Misty was sitting on the deck swinging her feet in the void between the wood and water below. I could tell from her red and swollen eyes that she'd been crying. Still, I had a hard time sympathizing with her. "He wants to apologize," I told her.

"That's sweet."

I could tell from the look in her eyes that she was calculating whether he had any value to her. Sometimes it's hard not to take sides, even unintentionally. In this case I made a decision. If Kyler had a shot at turning this around, he didn't need to talk to her. "We're going to get you back to the mainland and checked out."

"What happens after that?"

I saw something else in her expression and thought of Allie, promising myself I would do everything in my power not to let her be faced with this kind of decision. Her current employment situation was over, but in Miami, for a girl with her looks, there were plenty of options, and most didn't ask for references. I knew there was nothing I could say to her that would help.

I left her there and returned to the house. The diver radioed his commander that the situation was diffused and to send two boats over. Seconds later, I heard engines start and looked out the window at the boats coming toward us. Grace was in the first, and I thought about letting her take Misty, but we had to deal with Billie. This battle might be over, but Billie was still out there and we needed a full statement from Kyler.

While I waited, I thought about Billie, probing my memory for every time I had seen him and how he acted. At the dock party, he had been the most boisterous and I had assumed then he was either drunker than the rest or he had a larger-than-life personality. His behavior on the field should have sent a red flag. When he had backed into coverage, tipped, and intercepted a ball, I had thought it a pretty athletic move for a kid his size. Then I remembered his celebration: prancing around and mocking his teammates, it had taken several whistles to stop him.

The boats were approaching. I waved Grace off and motioned for the second boat to dock. There were three officers aboard. Two held the boat to the dock, while one helped Misty aboard. The testosterone must have boosted her spirits and she went quietly. Honestly, I hoped this was the last I saw of her, but I doubted it. I watched them leave and noticed her body language as she flirted with the deputies.

After the boat was a safe distance from the pier, I waved Grace over. They docked, and I called inside for the boy to come out with his hands above his head. Grace cuffed him and read him his Miranda rights. He was helped aboard, followed by the diver. I climbed aboard last. "Can you get him in an interrogation room and call the DA?" I asked. "He's not the killer." The engine drowned out our conversation as we idled over to the structure where my boat was docked. I had decided to let Miami-Dade have the small fish and save the turf war for Billie.

26

When we reached the dock, I jumped out of the boat, and after agreeing to meet Grace at the station, ran toward the park service boat for my phone. Blood pounded in my ears from the adrenaline and anxiety and I tried to take a deep breath before pressing the *home* button. The screen was littered with alerts and messages from Martinez. He must have heard the SWAT call and was sitting in his office watching everything unfold on his screens. My hand trembled as I scrolled past his messages and found one from Justine: *Need you ASAP.*

I stopped reading and pressed the phone icon in the header. It was hard to hear her over the background noise, and when I first heard the voice on the other end, I had to glance at the screen to see if it was the right number.

"Dad?"

My heart flipped. "Allie?" I tried to recover. "Hey!"

"Hey to you, too."

There was so much I wanted to ask and tell her I didn't know where to start. "Where are you guys?"

"Some restaurant with your girlfriend." She lowered her voice. "She's pretty cool, Dad."

My eyes started to water. "Can I speak to her? I'll head right over."

"Hey!" Justine said. "She's nice."

This was going too well and I wondered if Jane, my ex was with them, though I couldn't imagine a scenario where she wasn't. "Where are you guys? I'm heading back now."

She gave me the name of a restaurant on the river with a dock. I thanked her, and put the phone away. Whatever speed I had gotten out of the boat before was exceeded by at least ten knots as it flew over the water. Twenty minutes later, I entered the river and had to slow. My phone couldn't figure out whether I was walking, driving, or on a bus, but I found the restaurant. It took all the restraint I had to slow down, drop the fenders, and check the current. I wanted to slam into the dock and run to my daughter—and Justine.

I was on the dock when I saw her coming toward me and stood up with the end of the bow line still in my hand. She had grown over the year since I had last seen her. Fathers always thought their daughters were beautiful and she was every bit of that. I dropped the line and walked to her. I would have run, except she was only ten feet away. Lifting her off her feet, I hugged her tightly and could feel the intensity returned. "I'm so glad to see you," I said, pushing myself back to look at her.

The little girl look was gone, replaced my mascara and some blush and I thought of Misty for a brief second. "Where's your mom and Justine?"

"Up there, come on." The little girl was back as she took my hand and led me to the table.

I had been more anxious about seeing Jane than Allie. It's an odd thing after spending sixteen years with someone to find yourself on the other side of the fence. But I knew our breakup wasn't about the usual suspects—sex and money—the classic relationship destroyers. Ours had been my work and the threat of bodily harm to her and Allie. I never blamed her for her actions, only the extent to which she took them. The other fear of divorced dads now confronted me head on.

The round table buffered the lines between the two women. They sat across from each other, but the way they were leaning over and talking made them appear close—too close. Allie provided the necessary barrier by sitting between them. "Hi, Jane," I said, not knowing what else to say to my ex who I'd just forced to appear in court. I leaned in and kissed Justine on the cheek and set my hand on her shoulder.

"Hi, Kurt," Jane said.

"Allie looks great." The small talk continued and I wondered where this was going. I was dying to talk to Justine about the hearing. As if sensing something, Jane rose and excused herself.

I held out my hands once she was out of sight. "Wow, I never expected this."

"She's not so bad. The judge ordered mediation, so it wasn't that big a deal that you weren't there. Jane knows she has to give you some visitation, but you'll have to appear yourself for that one."

"But, now?"

"She's quite a girl. After the hearing she asked to see you."

"It's a huge deal and I don't know how to thank you."

She winked and shifted her eyes to Allie. I squeezed her shoulder and turned to my daughter. "Come on, tell me everything."

Dinner went by in a blur, and I realized when Justine tapped my arm and handed me my phone, that I hadn't touched my food or paid any attention to her or Jane. Grace's name was on the screen and I snapped back to reality. I answered and asked her to hold on while I excused myself and went to the railing.

"What's up?"

"This kid's ready to spill everything. The DA just met with his lawyer and cut a deal. As long as his story holds up, he'll get a break. He's not eighteen yet, so that's going to help the cause."

"Crap, I'm tied up with something." I glanced over at the table and saw a questioning look on Justine's face. "I'll get there as soon as I can."

I walked back to the table with a plan. "Hey, kiddo, can I talk to your mom for a minute?"

Allie gave her a questioning look and Jane nodded to her.

"Hey, I bet there are some tarpon cruising up under the dock. You wanna check them out?" Justine saved the day again.

The two walked away, leaving me alone with Jane for the first time in over a year. "You look good," I said. I was going to ask if she needed anything, but I knew she cashed my rather large checks every month. With no expenses, at least for now, I hadn't fought the alimony and child support payments.

"Allie wants you in her life. I'm lukewarm, especially after today, but she's going to be eighteen in a few years and can make her own decisions then. If I'm not reasonable with her wishes, I could lose her."

That was classic Jane, always pragmatic. I almost wanted to tell her about Misty, but stopped myself. "I know she should be with you most of the time. She needs a stable place to live and go to school. I respect what you do for her."

"That's good to know. I think a few weekends and some holidays would work," she said. "I'm willing to try it, but you need to swear that she's not going to be in any danger."

I wanted to tell her what she wanted to hear, but before I could come up with words that would have at least some truth to them, my phone vibrated. I saw Grace's name and turned it over, but my ex knew me too well.

"At least try…"

27

I still had a sense of euphoria after seeing Allie, but it was time to focus. New waterways make me nervous, especially at night. The red and green placards were easily seen during the day. With the sun down and the moon below the horizon, it was a different story. The tide was running against the river's current and coupled with the wind blowing in off the water, the waves were stacked at the river's mouth requiring me to steer each one. Every year several boats capsized in conditions like this and Martinez would not be pleased if one had a park service logo on it.

Once we reached the main channel, I relaxed, turned to Justine, and put my arm around her. "I don't know how you did it...you're amazing." I kissed her hard on the lips and held it until I heard a horn sound from an oncoming boat.

Slowly, I watched the green and red navigation lights coming toward us and when there was a gap, I cut the wheel to port and headed toward South Beach. Grace had left a message to meet her at the marina there. I guessed she had sweated Kyler enough to arrest Billie. I looked ahead at the barrage of red and green lights, trying to sort the solid lights of the boat traffic from the blinking navigation markers. Between Justine, the chart plotter, and my own eyes, we had a hard time finding our way through the narrow cut between the mainland and Dodge Island. There was no wonder the port authority required pilots on the large freight ships.

Finally, I was in familiar territory and steered toward the lights of the marina. I started to relax again and moved closer to Justine, but just as I put my arm around her, a large wake rocked us as a boat blew past. This was supposed to be a no-wake zone and when I turned, I saw the boat heading toward the *no-motorized vessel* area off Virginia Key. I wasn't sure if it was something to worry about. This was Miami after all and this kind of behavior was far from unusual. I looked back to the mainland to see if a police vessel was in pursuit, but there were no lights heading our way. There was something familiar about the boat that had just passed and I spun my head hoping to catch a glimpse before it was out of sight.

I saw the name on the transom at the same time as my phone vibrated. It was Grace and I confirmed that the *Temptress* had just passed us. Billie must be on the run. There was nothing I could do in the small park service boat. He easily had twenty to thirty knots on me, even in the flat water. From his bio, I remembered he came from Venice, Louisiana. Growing up in the closest town to the mouth of the Mississippi and surrounded by miles of bayou country, he had ben born into a hunting and fishing community. I remembered hearing somewhere that the town had more boats than cars. I had no doubt he could run a boat and had no illusions he would make a mistake. The only thing I could do was turn toward the marina and find Grace. A text came through telling me there was a boat waiting there for me. She was already in pursuit.

I understood her quick reaction. The near-full moon had just broken the horizon and its light was already illuminating the water. With just the hint of a breeze, the seas were flat; one of the rare nights where a crossing of the Gulfstream was not only doable, but comfortable. There would be dozens of boats out tonight making the fifty-mile transit to the Bahamas—too many to distinguish one from another on radar. A visual was the only way we were going to identify him.

I saw the police boat just after I put my phone down. After slowing for the wake, I pushed down the throttle and headed toward the closest pier at the marina. A helicopter buzzed over just as we pulled up to the dock. There was an awkward moment when Kyler's sister helped us dock, but she passed a quick thank you for helping out her brother before we stepped across to the waiting Contender.

We introduced ourselves and got a ten-second safety briefing, mostly comprised of sit down and shut up, while one of the deputies tossed the lines onto the dock. The captain pulled away quickly and hit the button for the light bar. I moved next to him. "Wouldn't it be better to come up on them without them knowing who we are?"

"Shit, boy, you're takin' all the fun outta this."

If I thought it couldn't get worse than Dick Tracy, I was wrong. I studied the captain as he chewed on a toothpick and hit the switch anyway. The two toothpick-chewing deputies with him were smirking and I was sure they would all be smoking cigars if we weren't aboard.

He ignored my request and kept the lights on. I had to admit it was effective, at least for the time being. This time of day, the traffic was mixed between recreational boaters enjoying the evening and commercial boats heading in and out. They all moved to the side, respecting the authority of the police boat. Ignoring them, I searched the horizon for the *Temptress*. The Contender was up on plane and we were about a hundred yards from the end of the breakwater when I saw a likely target.

Moving closer to the captain, I pointed out a boat ahead. He winked at me and cut the lights as if this were his plan all along. I grabbed a pair of binoculars sitting on top of the console and scanned the water, focusing on the boat until a container ship being towed by two tugs came between us and blocked the horizon. I was so focused on trying to find the *Temptress* that I hadn't even noticed it. Now it was becoming relevant very quickly as it approached.

Our captain hit the siren, blasting several quick warnings to the larger boat, but not moving it out of the way. The pilot boat escorting the ship was just across from us now and I saw the man at the helm wave his hands frantically in our direction. Ships this large were severely limited in maneuverability, especially the ability to stop quickly. Depending on their speed, it could take as much as a half-mile for one to stop. The pilot held a microphone, which he was screaming unheard words into. I looked over at the captain of the police boat and saw only a grin. He was ignoring the pilot's warning and I thought he was going to flip him off. Finally, at the last minute, he crossed directly behind the boat. I was thrown off balance when we slammed over its wake forcing me to scramble for one of the seats by the transom.

The captain continued through the cut into open water and after passing the last marker, turned back toward the boat I had indicated. We had lost so much time that its anchor light was just a dot on the horizon. Even with the pair of three-hundred-horsepower engines on her stern, the Contender was no match for the boat ahead of us. The captain thought otherwise, and, once we reached open water, ignoring the mile-long wake of the container ship, we suddenly accelerated. Not trusting the captain, I grabbed for whatever I could and reached the helm where I grabbed the binoculars again.

The boat was too far away to read the name and, in any event, it was hidden by the three outboards hanging on her transom. I had never thought of the Contender as underpowered, but here we were. "He's running for open water," I yelled over the engine noise.

"No shit, Sherlock."

At first I thought Billie had seen the lights of the police boat and was headed for the imaginary three-mile line where the State's power ended and would then push it for another nine miles to reach International waters. The Bahamas lay only another thirty miles from there. Instead, the cowboy move of playing chicken with the freighter had actually hidden our pursuit. Now that I knew where Billie was headed, I went back to the seat by the transom.

Pulling out my phone, I pecked out a message to Grace. It would have been easier to call, but the engine noise forced me to text and ask her for her position. They were miles to the south. There were too many options out here. North would take you up the coast to Palm Beach where it was a quick shot to Grand Bahama. Straight ahead lay

Bimini and to the south were the Keys—a hundred islands that a boat could get lost in. I updated her on our position and asked if she had seen anything. The answer came back negative. Watching the anchor light ahead, I wondered how far offshore Miami-Dade would chase the boat. We were probably at or close to the three-mile state limit and the federal waters only extended another six miles. If he was running for the Gulfstream and the Bahamas, we would need a faster boat.

I slid back to the bench seat by the transom and sat next to Justine thinking about my options. Johnny Wells came to mind, and I pecked out a quick text to my friend at ICE. Using the premise that the *Temptress* was making a run for it, I asked for his help. ICE had the authority that Miami-Dade lacked—and their thirty-nine-foot Interceptor with its four three-hundred-horsepower engines was one step higher on the bad-ass boat ladder.

My phone vibrated and I looked down at the screen. My Hail Mary had worked. He had found us on radar and was close by and happy to assist. Working my way back to the helm, I yelled to the captain that ICE was on their way. Instead of dropping power, he looked away and pushed the throttles to their max. The boat, already cruising at close to forty knots, edged closer to fifty.

"Not in our county," he yelled back.

A pissing contest was not going to stop Billie and I tried to think of a way to persuade him. As it turned out, I didn't need to. Coming straight at our starboard side was the Interceptor. The captain cursed, but knew he was outgunned, both in engine power and authority. He backed off on the throttle and glared at me. I was making more enemies than friends. Before I could respond, the Interceptor had fenders out and pulled to our side.

Both Johnny Wells and the captain of the Miami-Dade boat were trained in off-loading passengers and cargo at sea and the exchange started smoothly. Justine jumped nimbly across, and I started after her until the last second when I heard the pitch of the Contender's engine rise just slightly. The boats shifted. I had braced myself, having expected some kind of ploy by the captain and had been ready. In the split second between when I heard the engine and the propeller bit the water, I jumped across. Before I could catch his eye, the Miami-Dade boat had turned and seconds later was up on plane, heading back to port.

"Appreciate it," I said to Johnny.

"No worries. I know that ass. Figured even if you were full of it about chasing down the boat, I could at least save you from him."

I searched the open water ahead of us. In the time needed to make the exchange, we had lost visual on the *Temptress*. Johnny didn't panic, instead he looked down at his instruments and I followed his gaze to the radar screen.

"There she is."

28

Johnny Wells and his guys were pros. I had originally met the ICE crew during a drug bust down near the southern boundary of the park and, unlike my relationship with Miami-Dade, ours was comfortable.

Johnny had the dot on the radar locked into the autopilot and we discussed how to take down the boat. Although I was included in the conversation, he wasn't looking for advice, but rather wanted to know about our adversary—what he had for boating experience and weapons. I gave him some background on Billie. Growing up in bayou country, he was likely to be proficient with firearms and we had already seen him run a boat. His emotional condition might be unstable and I gave Johnny a quick character sketch from what I had seen of him at the party and on the field. Orders were passed to the three other members of the crew, then Justine and I were issued bulletproof vests. After sliding mine over my head, and checking Justine's, I looked ahead to see the faint white glow of the *Temptress's* mast light ahead.

I added the horsepower in my head. The *Temptress* had three two-hundred horsepower engines hanging from her transom. Alex and Rosen had hung them there to lure recruits, not outrun the Interceptor with four, two-twenty-fives. I was pretty sure the narrow beam of the Interceptor as well as the skill of the captain and crew would add to our advantage. Billie, not suspecting that we were this close, was also in cruise mode. Thinking he had evaded the pursuit, if he were running to the Bahamas, he would be throttled back to conserve fuel. We came up on him fast.

Justine and I were on either side of Johnny at the helm as we approached. I thought it was going to happen quickly, but Billie must have seen us coming and I saw the white wash behind the *Temptress* flare up as his boat accelerated. Now we would see who had the faster vessel. The race was short-lived when I saw the muzzle flash from the *Temptress* and a second later, fiberglass shards flew from the bow of the Interceptor. Johnny's face tightened and he swerved to starboard in an evasive maneuver. Without having to call out an order, the crew immediately took defensive positions. He hit a switch, which activated the light bar. There was no doubt now that Billie knew who was behind him. Shots continued to come from the *Temptress* though there was no indication that any more had hit.

"Get the RPG out," Johnny called to one of his men and turned to me. "Show and tell time." He picked up the microphone. "Vessel on our port side. This is ICE. Heave to and prepare to be boarded." He turned the volume up awaiting a reply. There was nothing but static and the boat's course and speed remained unchanged. "Bastard," Johnny cursed under his breath.

The water changed and I knew we had crossed the invisible line into the Gulfstream. The six-knot river running offshore through the Atlantic Ocean was pushing against the wind, creating standing waves where the two currents collided. We crossed into the Stream and Johnny, knowing the waters, used the swells to our advantage. Instead of following behind the *Temptress,* he ran alongside. I wondered how long this was going to go on. A glance at the chart-plotter showed the several small islands ahead. Bimini, was only miles away. If the chase carried us into Bahamian waters, we would have no authority.

"What are we going to do?" I asked, knowing he already had an answer.

"Watch this," he said, calling to the man on the bow to fire.

An orange stream flashed from the weapon as the RPG flew toward the *Temptress*. I worried for a second that there would be no arrest.

"First one's over the bow," Johnny said. He waited until the projectile crossed in front of the other boat and picked up the microphone again. "Vessel to our port. This is your last warning."

There was a hesitation aboard the other boat now that he knew he was outgunned. It slowed and the chase was over.

"Had to wait until we were in international waters to use that one. Too much paperwork in federal waters."

It seemed the bureaucracy continued through Homeland Security. "As long as we get him."

The *Temptress* was dead in the water and the ICE agents worked like a well-oiled machine to take the boat. Within a few minutes we were tied up alongside and Billie was face down on the deck straddled by an agent who quickly had him in cuffs. The other men cleared the cabins.

29

Grace met us on the docks and took Billie into custody. "Billie is your arrest. You'll need to come down to the station."

Justine was beside me now. "You go do what you need to. I'll hang outside," she kissed me on the cheek.

Without a vehicle, I rode with Grace to the station where Billie was run through processing. It turned out that he was eighteen and would have to face the charges as an adult. I wasn't wanting to judge the merits of our justice system, deciding if on a certain day, someone should face trial as a child or adult, but after what Billie had done, there had to be some punishment.

Alex and Rosen were both in the waiting room and came toward me when I exited the locked door. Rosen was more concerned about the boat than Billie or his victims. Alex was slightly humbled. I wasn't sure if he understood he was part of the process of destroying young men and marginalizing young women. He had to know the NCAA would be called in and his party would be over.

The lawyers and reporters filed in just as I was leaving. Martinez would be here soon, making sure he was front and center at the podium. I walked out the doors of the station and saw Justine parked at the curb.

"Hey! Need a lift?"

I smiled and got into her car. We sat in silence for a moment while I tried to let the events of the last few days fall off me. Some said that a case was over as soon as the cell door slammed. It wasn't that way for me. It took me a while to process what happened to the victims and people like Misty, whose lives, some for the better, and others for the worse, had been changed by the crime. I thought of Misty and hoped this would be a wake up call and get her on a better path.

"Breakfast?" Justine asked.

"Nope," I said.

"Works for me," she said, and pulled away from the curb.

We had breakfast in bed several hours later and decided to move out to Adams Key for a few days. I'm sure Martinez would approve my request for a few days off if I didn't run the overtime for the past week through the system, and Justine had sick days accumulated.

It took me the whole day and most of the next to finally unwind. We woke to a brilliant morning, though I knew it was another step towards summer when the nighttime temperatures wouldn't drop below eighty for several months. I sat there drinking my coffee, thinking about what we should do and the one thing from the case that hadn't faded.

"I want to dive," I said.

"Nice. That little snorkeling excursion did it for you," she said.

I had told her about the swim over to the house. "Yeah, maybe something Allie would like, too."

"I think that's awesome. How about I call TJ down in Key Largo and see if he'll take us out on one of those discover diving trips. You don't have to be certified for those."

I smiled. "Won't I drag you down?"

"Nah, I just like blowing bubbles sometimes. Let's do it."

Several hours later, we were at the docks of TJ and Alicia's dive shop in Key Largo. I had met the couple before, in my first case here helping out Mac Travis. We embraced like old friends and TJ took me aside to run me through the pre-dive briefing. Alicia and Justine disappeared upstairs.

"You two seem good together," TJ said.

"Yeah," I said, fiddling with the regulator. I'd been thinking about how things had moved forward with our relationship and was almost ready for the next step. But, then with Allie coming into our lives, I wasn't sure I should rush. "You think you could teach my daughter to dive?"

"It's what I do, dude. Happy to."

I had a vision of the three of us as sort of a family—diving together. "That'd be great," I said, and smiled at Justine who was coming down the stairs.

"What are you so happy about?" she asked.

"Just stuff. Let's do this," I said, hoping it wasn't the last time I spoke those words to her.

Get the next book in the Kurt Hunter Mystery Series
Would you commit a murder if no one was watching?

Congress can't pass a budget and Biscayne National Park is paying the price. With Special Agent Kurt Hunter out of work, two rivals gangs start a turf war in the park. But when a body is found hanging from the railing of the iconic Boca Chita Lighthouse, Kurt refuses to sit back and fish while the gangs take over his park.

Lies and deceit run rampant through the gangs forcing Kurt deep into the labyrinth of Miami's counterculture to solve the murder.

Get it now!

Thanks For Reading

If you liked the book please leave a review here

For more information please check out my web page:
https://stevenbeckerauthor.com/

Or follow me on Facebook:
https://www.facebook.com/stevenbecker.books/

I'm also on Instagram as: stevenbeckerauthor

**Get my starter library First Bite for Free!
when you sign up for my newsletter**

http://eepurl.com/-obDj

First Bite contains the first book in each of Steven Becker's series:

- **Wood's Reef**
- **Pirate**
- **Bonefish Blues**

By joining you will receive one or two emails a month about what I'm doing and special offers.

Your contact information and privacy are important to me. I will not spam or share your email with anyone.

Wood's Reef

"A riveting tale of intrigue and terrorism, Key West characters in their *full glory! Fast paced and continually changing direction Mr Becker has me hooked on his skillful and adventurous tales from the Conch Republic!"*

Pirate
"A gripping tale of pirate adventure off the coast of 19th Century Florida!"

Bonefish Blues*"I just couldn't put this book down. A great plot filled with action. Steven Becker brings each character to life, allowing the reader to become immersed in the plot."*

Get them now (http://eepurl.com/-obDj)

Also By Steven Becker

Kurt Hunter Mysteries

Backwater Bay

Backwater Channel

Backwater Cove

Backwater Key (May 2018)

Mac Travis Adventures

Wood's Relic

Wood's Reef

Wood's Wall

Wood's Wreck

Wood's Harbor

Wood's Reach

Wood's Revenge

Wood's Betrayal

Tides of Fortune

Pirate

The Wreck of the Ten Sail

Haitian Gold

Will Service Adventure Thrillers

Bonefish Blues

Tuna Tango

Dorado Duet

Storm Series

Storm Rising

Storm Force